CRIMEWORKS BRUIN

KNOCK THREE-ONE-TWO

Published by
Bruin Books, LLC
April, 2010

This book was designed and edited by Jonathan Eeds

Graphics design by Michelle Roper

Printed in the United States of America

ISBN 978-0-9826339-1-5

Bruin Books, LLC
Eugene, Oregon, USA

www.bruinbookstore.com

KNOCK THREE— ONE— TWO

FREDRIC BROWN

Bruin Books
The Emerald Empire
Eugene, Oregon

5:00 P.M.

He had a name, but it doesn't matter; call him *the psycho.*
That's what the newspapers and everyone who read them called
him now, since his second murder two months ago. At first he'd
been called by various designations: insane rapist-killer, homi-
cidal maniac, sexual psychopath, and others. For convenience, for
shorthand, it had boiled down to the psycho. The police called
him that too, although they had been moving heaven and earth
to find a better name for him, a name like Peter Jones or Robert
Smith, a name that would let them find and apprehend him
before he killed again. And again.

And now tonight the Need was on him again. The need to
rape and kill a woman.

He stood in the hallway of an apartment building, before a
door. Nervous tension was making him flex and unflex his
hands—his tremendously strong, strangler's hands that had
already killed twice and, if everything went well, were about to
kill again. He forced himself to hold them still. Not that it
mattered here and now, with no one watching him, but it was a
habit that had been growing on him and one that he had to
break, lest he forget sometime and do it when people were
watching him and make them wonder about him, about why he
did it. And maybe go on wondering from there; in this city right
now just about everybody was watching his neighbor suspi-
ciously, watching for just such little signs as that.

He took a deep breath and then raised a hand and knocked on
the door. A light, almost diffident knock, not a peremptory one.

He heard the click of high heels coming to the door. And her
voice called out, "Yes? Who is it?"

He sensed her just beyond door and saw the sliver of her
shadow reflected on the hardwood flooring.

He made his voice as soft as his knock had been, and as unfrightening, just loud enough to carry to her. "Western Union, ma'am. Collect telegram, from Pittsburgh."

Collect of course, so she couldn't ask him to slide, it under the door. And the "from Pittsburgh" should allay any suspicion she might have, since that's where her husband had gone yesterday, on a business trip. She might wonder why he'd wire her collect—but there could be reasons for that.

He heard the knob turn and tensed himself, ready. Then the door opened—a few inches, on a chain—and knew that he had failed. He threw himself back flat against the wall alongside the door so she wouldn't get a glimpse of him.

And ran, down the flight of stairs and out to the street. Thank God her apartment was a back one and didn't have a window on the street from which she could still get a look at him. Once out the door he forced himself to walk slowly to his car. He got in and drove away, being careful not to drive too fast or too slow.

What a hell of a lousy break. He'd checked that apartment three days ago and there hadn't been a chain bolt on the door then. Her husband must have put it on for her just before he left on his business trip.

Well, at least he had got away safely.

He was five blocks off and had just turned into a main traffic artery when he heard the sound of squad car sirens converging on the building he had just left.

5:02 P.M.

After his wife had left, Ray Fleck paced the flat in rage and despair. With rage, at first, predominating. Damn her, damn her, he thought. What kind of wife would flatly refuse to help her husband when he was in a jam, a real jam? The bitch, she could give him the money so easily, and never feel it. All she had to do was cash in that accursed insurance policy. What did she need it for? A policy on *herself.* And it had a cash surrender value of over three thousand dollars— maybe almost four thousand by now; several payments had been made since they'd last argued about it.

Or she could at least borrow against it, and all he needed was five hundred bucks. Four hundred and eighty, to be exact, but he'd made it a round figure. But no, that damned policy of hers was sacrosanct; she wouldn't even borrow against it. Sacrosanct for what, for God's sake? Sure it was her savings, her stake, and she'd taken it out herself, had started saving that way, before they were married. But now that she *was* married and had a husband to support her, why should she feel she needed a stake? Unless she was planning to leave him, or thinking that she might decide to do so— that was possible. They had had some pretty bitter quarrels, the past two years out of the three they'd been married. But she'd fought to keep that policy even during the first year, and they'd been pretty happy at first. He'd been in a lucky streak, riding high, and they'd both been in love. Women love you when you're in the chips. When it comes to money, women
are a one-way street. You can spend it on them, but try to get some of it back. Just try.

Besides, some of the money in that policy was his, rightfully his. Hadn't he, for most of that first year, given her money to pay the premiums on it? Under protest, of course; he'd tried to talk her out of wanting to keep on carrying it. "Honey," he'd said, "what do we want a policy on *you* for? I don't want you to die, but if you should die I don't want ten grand out of it." But she'd had an answer for that. Women always have an answer.

"Ray, darling," she'd said, "I'd agree with you if this were just an insurance policy—but it isn't. It's a ten-year endowment policy, and that's a way of saving. A good way. I've carried it for over four years now and in less than another six years we'll have ten thousand dollars in cash. Won't that be nice?"

"Yeah, but it's a long time away—and those are damn high premiums. I feel like a pauper saving crumbs in a paper bag. Why short ourselves now to have money when we're old? What good will ten thousand do us then? Now's the time to enjoy it—while we're still young."

She laughed. "We won't exactly be old in six years. I'll be twenty-nine and you'll be thirty-five. As to what we can use it for—a house, if we haven't already bought one by then. It doesn't have to be big or expensive, but I want us to have a home of our own someday; I don't want to live in furnished flats the rest of my life. Or if we already have our own home by then, maybe it would be enough to let you start in business for yourself; you've said you would like to, if you had capital."

That made sense to him. Not the part about "a home of our own"; he was a city dweller and wouldn't live in a house in the suburbs if somebody gave him one, but he could talk her out of that idea when the time came.

But with ten thousand capital, all at once, he *could* do himself a lot of good. He was a liquor salesman and seldom made less than a hundred a week in commissions: he averaged considerably higher than that. He worked for J. & B. Liquor Distributors, and he had a good following among taverns and liquor stores all over the city. And he had at least some contacts with salesmen for wholesalers and distillers; they knew he was a good salesman. If he could set himself up as an independent distributor, make a profit on what he sold instead of just a commission, he'd be on his way toward making big money instead of peanuts. But it would be a long, slow pull. He'd need capital, all right.

He'd made only one more effort. "But wouldn't it be better to put that much money in the bank instead? Then if there was an emergency, we could get at it easier."

But Ruth had shaken her head firmly. "We *could* put money in the bank, but you know you wouldn't, most weeks. Having regular premiums to meet will *make* us save. And if an emergency comes up we can borrow against the policy— and get the money the same day, since the company has an office here. But, Ray, I'd do it only for a real emergency— an accident or serious illness, an operation, something like that. Not to let you bet heavily on a horse race because you've got a hot tip, or to let you pay off a gambling debt if you run in the hole."

Well, she'd warned him. But he'd given in, and had given her money to keep up the premiums for a while, ten or eleven monthly premiums. Then he'd run into a streak of bad luck instead of good and had told her he couldn't give her the money; he just didn't have it to give.

She'd taken it calmly. "All right, Ray. But I'm *not* going to cash in that policy. I'll take a job, part time anyway, and make enough to pay the premiums myself. More than that, I hope."

And she had taken a job, and had worked ever since. He hadn't objected. Why should he? If the damn policy meant that much to her, why shouldn't she earn the money to keep it up? And, for that matter, to kick in on household expenses or at least to buy her own clothes? Why should he have to earn everything for both of them and let her do nothing?

She'd held several jobs. Checker at a supermarket, ticket seller at a movie. Currently, and for the past eight or nine months, she was working an evening shift as a waitress in a Greek restaurant. Thirty hours a week, from five-thirty to eleven-thirty five nights a week. Usually when he was home at this time he drove her to work—and sometimes when he was doing nothing important around eleven-thirty, picked her up after her work. But this afternoon he'd had to leave his car at a garage to have some work done on it (that would be another damn bill on top of everything else) so the question hadn't arisen. Just as well, since they'd quarreled so bitterly. They'd probably have kept on quarreling in the car, and it would have done him no good. He recognized by now that he'd lost the argument; she was adamant and she'd stay that way. She hadn't believed him when he'd told her he was in physical danger.

Well, he didn't really believe that himself. Joe Amico was tough but he wasn't a gangster, and he wasn't going to risk having anybody killed for four hundred and eighty bucks.

True, he might go to the length of having someone beat up a little if he thought the guy was welshing on him, didn't even *intend* to pay off. But Joe knew him better than that. He'd owed Joe before and had always paid off—although never anything like almost five hundred bucks; *how* had it ever run that high? Joe knew he had a good job and was good for the money eventually.

All he needed was a lucky streak, and he was due for one. Overdue for one. At poker, maybe, if the horses kept running badly for him. Sometimes when the horses ran badly the cards ran well for him. And vice versa.

There was a poker game tonight that might do the trick, if he had or could raise enough of a stake to sit in on it. Yes, this was Thursday night, and Harry Brambaugh always had a Thursday night poker game at his place. From eleven o'clock on, sometimes well into the next day. But—

Although he knew approximately how much money he had, he took out his wallet and counted it. Twenty-eight bucks, twenty-eight lousy bucks. Not enough to sit in on a game at Harry's. He ought to have a hundred to start with to buck that game, not a stake that could go in the first pot he got into beyond the ante. But if he could raise a hundred—well, a lucky streak could easily run it to enough to let him pay off Joe Amico and maybe some left over.

Raising a hundred didn't sound nearly as impossible as raising four hundred and eighty. Even if he had to borrow ten bucks apiece from ten guys. With all evening to do it in.

The phone rang. He picked it up and said "Ray Fleck."

And then recognized the voice that said "Hi, Ray," and wished he'd let the phone ring. It was Joe Amico.

He said, "Listen, Joe, I haven't been able to do anything yet—but I'm working on it. I'll raise it somehow, pretty soon. I'm sorry, but you know I'm good for it."

"I know you're good for it. You'd better be. But I want you to drop in and see me this evening."

"Sure, Joe, if you want me to. I'm coming downtown anyway. But it won't do any good. I'm flat."

"Flat or not, you come in. I'll be here till ten. Any time between now and then. Got me?"

"Okay, Joe. I'll see you."

He sighed as he put down the phone. Well, he was going downtown anyway; that had been the truth. And probably Joe was going to give him an ultimatum, a time limit. And it would be an unpleasant interview but at least he'd know the worst. He'd know how long he had to raise the money. Or whether Joe would take it in weekly payments if he simply couldn't raise it any other way. He'd hate that; he'd hate it like hell. Because, for a hell of a long time, it would leave him no surplus to do any betting with. And his luck was due to change; it *had* to change.

He strolled to the front window and stood looking down at the street, wondering whether he should go downtown now and eat whenever he got hungry, or save himself money by rustling something to eat here before he left. Since Ruth had to leave for work at five he had to fend for himself or eat out the five evenings she worked, but he didn't mind that; sometimes he enjoyed cooking simple things for himself, and of course she did the cleaning up and dishwashing the next morning.

Aside from that he was glad she worked an evening shift; in fact, he'd talked her into doing it. He was out almost every evening himself; he'd explained to her that it was his best time for selling. And that was partly true. Some of his bar owner customers delegated the duller daytime hours to a bartender who wasn't authorized to do any buying and themselves took over the bar, with or without the help of a bartender or two, during the evening hours. Even tonight he should probably make a business call or two, although he didn't feel in the mood to do it. Just downtown bars, of course, since he wouldn't have his car till tomorrow. Yes, he could see Harry Webber and Chuck Connolly; they were both due to be called on.

Brakes squealed in the street below and his eyes swiveled toward the source of the sound, the nearby corner. It was a near accident. A kid, a boy about ten, had run across the street right in front of an oncoming car and the driver had slammed on his brakes and skidded, had managed to stop with only inches to spare. A close thing, a very close thing. But the kid ran on and the driver must have been the more shaken up of the two; he sat there almost a minute before starting up the car again.

Accidents can happen, even though this one didn't. And unbidden a thought rose in Ray Fleck's mind. What if an accident should happen to Ruth, on her way to work right now or on her way home tonight? Not that she'd run in front of a car like that crazy kid had, but pedestrians can be hit even when they're not at fault. By a drunken driver or a driver who loses control of his car. Sometimes cars even ran up onto a sidewalk and—

Oh, the chances of anything like that happening, of Ruth being killed, were a million to one against. Pretty poor odds— but good God, wouldn't it be a perfect answer to his problem, to all his problems, if it *should* happen? As beneficiary of her policy he'd have ten thousand dollars, ten whole grand, all at once. What he owed Arnico would be peanuts; he'd still have nine and a half grand. It would be enough; he could make the break right—away. He'd no longer be Ray Fleck, liquor salesman, but Ray Fleck, Distributor. And on the way to a real income and plenty of respect.

Funny he'd never thought seriously about the possibility of his ever collecting that ten grand as a beneficiary. Maybe because Ruth was such a healthy girl; she hadn't been sick a day in the three years of their marriage. But even a healthy person can have an accident.

Or— He pushed that thought aside. He was no angel and he'd done a lot of dishonest things in his life, but he wasn't a murderer. Even if he was he'd never get away with it. If a woman is killed her husband is always the prime suspect, even if he hasn't any insurance on her.

Forget it, he told himself, and forgot it. Abruptly he made up his mind not to stick around the flat until he got hungry enough to eat here, to save a buck. What was a buck in the jam he was in? And the sooner he got downtown the more chances he'd have to raise a stake to get in that poker game with at eleven. The game that was the only chance he knew of to win any real money tonight. The game he *had* to get into.

He left the flat, walked down the two flights of stairs and out to the street. He was lucky; a taxi was going by and he flagged it and got in. Downtown was only a short cab ride, half a buck plus tip, and he hated waiting for buses. "Main and Willis," he told the driver. "Drop me off at the northwest corner."

That was the corner where Benny had his newsstand and his first stop would be to pick up a Racing Form. Not that he'd be placing any bets tonight—or tomorrow unless he won really big at poker, but he always liked to study the Form anyway and do his handicapping. Besides Benny always—when he remembered; Benny's memory wasn't too good—held out a Form for him and if Benny had, he didn't want to leave him stuck with it. Poor Benny. Crazy Benny, some people called him; but Ray didn't think he was really crazy, just a little lacking upstairs, prone to forgetting things. And sometimes (Ray had heard, although he'd never run into this himself) to remembering things that hadn't really happened. But he ran the newsstand all right and never made a mistake in making change.

He paid off the taxi and strolled to the wooden enclosure from which Benny sold his papers. "Hi, Benny," he said. "Remember to hold a Form for me?"

"Sure, Mr. Fleck. I *always* remember to." And this time Benny really had remembered. He reached behind him and took a copy of the Racing Form down from a shelf at the back of the stand.

Ray put down the coins to pay for it and picked it up, started to fold it as he turned, then had a sudden thought and turned back. Since he was going to have to raise his poker stake by borrowing a little each from as many friends as he could put the bite on, why not start here and now by seeing if Benny was good for a sawbuck? He'd never borrowed anything from Benny before, but what was to lose trying.

"Benny," he said. "I'm a little short on dough, wonder if you could lend me ten bucks. Just till Saturday, day after tomorrow, when I get my commission check."

Benny's big moon face didn't show any surprise. He said, "Why—why, I guess I can, Mr. Fleck." He took from under the counter the cigar box in which he kept bills—coins he kept in a change dispenser on his belt—and opened it. There were quite a few bills in it and for a second Ray considered whether he should ask if Benny could make it twenty instead; then he saw that all of the bills he could see were singles and maybe all of them were. In fact apparently all of them were because Benny didn't fish through them to look for a ten or two fives; he started counting out ten singles, one at a time, with the slow carefulness with which he always counted money or made change. He handed the ten bills over and Ray stuffed them into his wallet. "Thanks, Benny."

"Mr. Fleck. I just thought uh somethin'. You'll have to mail that money to me. I won't be here Saturday."

"Sure. Taking a vacation, huh? You better give me an address to send it to."

"You won't need no address, Mr. Fleck. I mean, you'll know from the papers. I been thinkin' it over all day and made up my mind. I'm goin' to give myself up to the police, before I do anything more. Soon as I close up the stand tonight."

"What are you talking about, Benny? Before you do any more what?"

"You been readin' in the papers about this sex psycho—" He pronounced the *ch* as in checkers. "Psycho— whatever it is?"

"Psychopath. What about him?"

"I'm him, Mr. Fleck. I killed them two women."

Ray Fleck put his head back and laughed heartily. "Benny, you're cr— I mean, get that idea out of your head. You didn't kill those women. *I know.* You wouldn't hurt a rabbit, Benny."

He started chuckling as he turned and walked away.

Feeling a little ashamed of himself, too, for having laughed in Benny's face. But he hadn't really been laughing at Benny at all, although he'd never be able to explain that to poor Benny. He'd been laughing at the crazy fact, the ridiculous fact, that Benny had chosen to make his confession to the one and only person in the entire city—outside of the psychopathic killer himself—who could know and did know, immediately and certainly, that Benny, no matter how crazy he might be, was *not* the killer.

5:20 P.M.

George Mikos surveyed his domain, his restaurant, and found it good. Everything was set up and ready for the dinner hour. No customers at the moment, except for one man having coffee at the counter, but they'd start coming in soon. Only one waitress on duty at the moment, but Ruth Fleck would be coming in ten minutes, and he knew he could count on her getting there; Ruth was dependable.

He turned and went through the swinging door back to the kitchen, ducking his head a little as he did so. He was a big man, six feet two inches tall, and that doorway was an inch or so too short for him. When he'd first bought the restaurant he'd intended to have the doorway made higher but he hadn't got around to it and by now he was so used to ducking that it was completely automatic; he didn't even know he did it.

The cook was scraping the top of the range, but looked around as he heard George come through the door. "Everything under control?" George asked him. "Sure, George," the cook said.

"Fine. I'll be in my office a while. Give a yell for me if and when I might be needed, either back here or up front."

He went into the room, a fair-sized room, off the kitchen that served him as an office. He left the door ajar. The kitchen and restaurant noises, the banging of pots and the clatter of dishes and such, wouldn't bother him; he was conditioned to concentrate away from them. He was also conditioned to hear them and evaluate them subconsciously. To know, especially from the frequency with which waitresses called back orders, when things were getting busy enough so his help might be needed, even if the cook did not, as he suggested, give a yell for him.

He sat down at the oak typewriter desk. The type-writer was already raised into typing position. There was a sheet of paper in it, blank except for a numeral 3 at the top; it was to be the third page of a letter he'd started early in the afternoon.

Before resuming the letter he picked up the two pages of it he'd already written and reread them rapidly.

Dear Perry,

It was wonderful to hear from you again after lo, these many years (almost ten of them, isn't it?) since we roomed together at college. I'm so glad you happened to run into Walt, that he was able to give you my address.

Congratulations on having gone on to a Ps.D. And on having opened your own office as a consulting psychologist—in New York and on Park Avenue, no less; it must be really a happy hunting ground and if you're not coining money already you will be soon.

No, I have not continued my formal education. Nor do I intend to, any more. By now I yam what I yam, a Goddam Greek who runs a restaurant. But I read a lot, study some; I'm not letting my mind stagnate completely. I try to keep up with things. For instance I subscribe to and read the *Journal of Psychology,* even though—I realize now—I'll never be more than a layman in that field. And although about half of my reading is escape reading, the other half isn't; I read classics too. My knowledge of and taste in literature is far ahead of what it used to be in our college days.

As for keeping in shape, I go to a gym two, sometimes three, mornings a week. I still go in for Greco-Roman wrestling, when I can find an opponent, and I haven't found one here who can take me at it.

You want a description of my restaurant, what it's called, everything about it. Everything about it would be a large order and wouldn't interest you unless you think you might start one of your own, and I doubt if you have that in mind. But I'll give you a rough idea.

First, it's called '*Mikos*'; I don't go in for fancy names and have no intention of trying to hide the fact that a Greek runs it. It's small, but not tiny. Between counter and tables it will seat thirty people, and during rush hours, usually does seat that many or almost that many.

It'll never make a Duncan Hines's rating, but neither will anyone ever call it a Greasy Spoon; it's clean. Our forte is good food at reasonable prices.

I employ an average of ten people. Not that many all at once, of course; they work varying shifts, since we're open from 7A.M. till 11:30 P.M.

I myself come in at about 11 A.M., before the lunch hour, and stay until closing time. That sounds a long working day—twelve and a half hours—but don't let it fool you because I actually work only about half of the time. There's a fair-sized room off the kitchen which I've converted into a combination office and den. I do my bookkeeping here, write checks for bills and salaries, type menus, all that sort of thing, but that doesn't take over an average of four hours a day. The holidays are always busier, of course.

Another two or three hours a day I spend in the kitchen or up front, helping out wherever needed. Some days more than that if someone fails to show up and we're short handed. But other days things go smoothly and I'm not needed at all. Call it an average of two hours a day.

So you see my actual working day is about six hours; the rest of the time I'm around, in case of emergency or to solve problems if any arise, but in general my time is my own. I read or study or think. If for any reason I'm short on sleep I take naps. Or I write letters, as I'm doing now.

And so much for the restaurant, except for the most important thing about it: it makes money. More than I, as a bachelor with relatively simple tastes, can spend. I've been investing in land just outside the city limits to the west, and as the city is growing in that direction, and rapidly, the land is equally rapidly appreciating in value. So, within another five years—but I'm beginning to sound as though I'm bragging and I'll stop. Suffice it to say there is no wolf at my door.

You ask me how my love life is doing. Probably your question was facetious, but I'm going to give it an honest answer...

That was where the second page of the letter had ended. George Mikos turned to the typewriter to go on and then decided, before starting page 3 to take a look to make sure Ruth Fleck had shown up; it was just five-thirty, her starting time.

He went to the door and opened it wider, and had to look no farther. She was just about to pass it, coming from the closet where the employees hung their coats.

"Hello, Ruth," he said. And then, "Ruth, you've been crying. Is something wrong? Is there anything I can do? Can you come in and talk a moment?"

She hesitated. "I— There *is* something I'd like to ask you about, George. But please not now. Later, after the dinner rush, I'll be calmer and much more sensible."

She went on, without giving him a chance to say anything more, through the swinging door into the restaurant. George watched until it had swung shut behind her. Then he pushed his own door partly shut again and went back to the desk. This time he started typing...

Now, and for the first time in my life, at least since late adolescence, I am in love, deeply in love, and with a woman with whom I have not had an affair and with whom I don't want or intend to have an affair, even if I could. At least I have found the right woman for me and I want everything or nothing. I want to marry the girl.

There is a fly in the ointment; the fly is the husband she already has. I am trying to convince her to divorce him and to marry me. Offhand, this may sound reprehensible, but I do not think that it is, really. Her husband is, if I may change my entomological metaphor, a louse.

He is a liquor salesman; that's nothing against him, but there is plenty else that is. He is a compulsive, congenital gambler, mostly on the horses; he's the type of horse player who does his own handicapping and thinks he can beat the game, which of course he can't. He probably earns at least a hundred a week but spends, or rather loses, at least half of that gambling, for which reason his wife has to work—and works for me as a waitress. Most of the time he's broke and in debt, living on his next week's commission check.

I don't think he's brutal to Ruth (that's her name; his is Ray Fleck) physically. I almost wish he were, because I think that if he ever struck her she would leave him, which, of course, is what I want to happen.

I know quite a bit about him, including the fact that he is at least occasionally unfaithful to her—which in itself justifies to me my breaking up their marriage if I can.

No, I didn't tell Ruth anything about what I heard. I was afraid that, whether or not those reports would decide her to divorce Fleck, she'd be angry at me for having had the presumption to tell her. Besides for all I know she may already know or at least suspect that Fleck cheats on her. Wives, I am told, can usually tell. What's the opinion of a consulting psychologist on that?

But that's not what I really want to ask you about. It's about something that doesn't concern me personally.

We have among us here a rapist-killer, obviously a psychotic, who has already raped and killed two women. Raped and killed in that sequence; he is not a necrophile. His first rape-killing was about four months ago, his second two months ago. The interval between two crimes is hardly sufficient to establish a time interval. But if it does, if it takes him about two months to build up pressure to make him kill again, then he is about due to strike a third time. His method—

But wait. Before I give the details, such as they are, I'll tell you where I come in, and where you come in. The captain in charge of our homicide department is a friend of mine. He is understandably a very worried guy. He's been under pressure from the chief of police, the police commissioner, the newspapers and the public to get friend psychopath. He may get demoted if he doesn't. And he hasn't a single clue or lead. With the press is fueling the fire of fear on a daily basis the people of this good town are thoroughly rattled.

He knows, of course, that I majored in psychology and every time we see one another he heckles me to make deductions about the killer. Or even guesses. I've made a few, but I'm afraid that, whether they are correct or not, they're not very helpful on the practical level of police work.

Maybe you can do better. You've studied a lot more abnormal psychology than I have. Anyway, I'm going to toss you the few known facts about our psycho and ask if you can make any suggestions that I haven't already made. I'll pass them on to the captain. If you can come up with anything at all helpful, it may save a life, or several lives. Here goes:

Both victims were young housewives. Both were attracttive. Each was home alone (home was a house in one case, an apartment in the other) at the time of the attack. In one case the husband was out of town on business, in the other working a swing shift at an airplane parts factory.

In neither case was there any sign of forcible entry; the woman herself must have admitted him or at least opened the door for him.

Both women were knocked unconscious with a blow to the chin, then carried to a bed; their clothes were torn off them and they were raped, then strangled to death. Still, from the- lack of anything indicating a struggle, unconscious from the knockout. (Don't ask me how the autopsies could prove or even indicate that the rape preceded the strangling but my friend tells me that the medical examiner is absolutely certain, so I'm willing to take his word for it.)

Both crimes occurred in the evening. We happen to know the exact time of one of them: ten o'clock. This was the one who lived in an apartment. The couple who lived in the apartment under hers heard a thud at that hour; they're certain of the time because the husband was just switching channels on the television to get their favorite ten o'clock program. Knowing that their upstairs neighbor was home alone they looked at one another, each wondering whether she might have had a fall and need help. But before either spoke to the other they heard footsteps moving around and decided she was all right, that she'd either dropped something fairly heavy or had a fall that hadn't hurt her.

That was the first of the two murders. We don't know the time of the second one so accurately. The woman's body wasn't found until early the next afternoon when her husband returned from his business trip. After so many hours the M. E. could only say that death had occurred late the previous evening, probably between nine o'clock and midnight.

We know him to be a man of considerable strength, not only from the steam behind the knockout blows he struck but from the way in which he ripped the clothes from his victims after carrying them to a bed. One of the women was wearing a quilted house coat that zipped open about halfway down the front; he tore it the rest of the way, and quilted material does not tear easily.

From the speed and accuracy with which he struck the police theorize that he may be or may have been a boxer. Also, from his strength, they believe he is more likely to be a laborer than a white collar worker. I'll go along with both of these deductions as possibilities or probabilities and not as certainties. A man with no boxing experience but with good coordination and a little luck could have struck those blows. And if he has a good mind (except for its warp) and/or a good education he'd certainly be doing something better than manual labor.

So much for the physical side, and to the mental. First, I do not believe he is a moron. He must have cased those jobs and known that the woman would be alone at the time he came.

Otherwise he had incredible luck—and I refuse to credit the incredible. Also, he left no fingerprints at the scene of either crime; he either wore gloves or avoided touching any surface that would take them. A moron wouldn't think of fingerprints.

But to a more important point, the nature of his psychosis. I have a theory; I hope you'll be able to expand on it if you agree or to offer a better one if you disagree.

I believe that he fears women to a psychotic degree, and hates them because he fears them. Call him a womanophobe. And because of his fear of women he is self-conscious in the presence of one to the point of complete impotence, even if the woman is willing; only with an unconscious woman can he find an outlet for his sex drive. His reason for killing women after he has used them can be sheer psychopathic hatred, flaring to highest pitch with or immediately after the orgasm. Or it can be caution; a dead woman can't describe him or identify him. My guess is that his reason for killing is a mixture of both those reasons.

If this description of his psychosis is correct it is almost certain that he is a bachelor. I use the "almost" because he may have been married once; an early very bad marriage might have been the starting point of his psychosis. But, whether once married or not I'd say it's certain that he is not currently living with a woman. I don't think he could stand to be around one in his current state of mind.

And I'd say that it's probable that, if he has any choice of occupations, he's working at a job that brings him into as little contact with women as possible. And living at a Y.M.C.A., a men-only hotel or—if he makes enough money—in a bachelor apartment.

Those are only probabilities, though. He may be smart enough, and actor enough, to have perfectly normal business and social contacts with women. If that's true he's going to be a lot harder to catch.

Speaking of how smart he is, we'll have a strong indication of that if and when he attempts a third crime. If he tries the same modus operandi he used the first two times he'll show himself to be much more stupid than I think he is, Because that method simply won't work a third time.

The women of this city are scared, have been scared ever since the second crime. Women alone in a house or flat simply don't open the door, even by day, until and unless they're damned sure who's on the other side of it. Chain bolts have been selling so fast that the hardware stores keep reordering by air express and still can't quite keep up with the demand. And from the number of speakeasy-type peep-holes that have been made in doors you'd think we were back in the days of Prohibition again.

The scare has had an odd incidental effect on our economy. Normally, in a city this size, there are several hundred house-to-house sales-men and canvassers working. Here and now there are none. For the past two months, since the second rape-killing, they have been able to gain entry into such a small percentage of homes that they simply can't make a living. They've all had to move on elsewhere to greener pastures or switch to some other occupation. Even big outfits like Fuller and Watkins have closed their local offices—temporarily, they hope. And not only salesmen are affected, but mailmen—if they have a C.O.D. or a registered letter that must be signed for—bill collectors, deliverymen, meter readers, collectors for charity drives, what have you.

It's amazing what strange effect two crimes by a...

George Mikos paused to think out the rest of the sentence and in the pause heard his cook's voice: "Hey, George, better come out and give a hand."

"Coming," he called back. And came.

6:15 P.M.

He wasn't hungry, but Ray Fleck decided that he'd better eat. He'd slept late and had only coffee for breakfast, and only a light lunch. And this evening he'd had two drinks already in his quest for money to get him into the poker game; like as not he'd have to take at least a dozen more in the course of the evening, and if he wanted to be able to play good poker he'd damn well better lay a foundation of food under that dozen drinks.

The bad thing about the two drinks he'd already had was that he'd taken them in vain. Worse than in vain because instead of helping him, raise money they'd cost him the ten bucks he'd borrowed from Benny and had put his slender capital back where it had been before. He'd seen through the window of the Palace Bar that Dick Johnson was there; Dick was usually a soft touch and he went inside and bellied up the bar beside Dick. He tried to buy him a drink, but Dick beat him to it by signaling the bartender with two upraised fingers, so Ray waited until he'd had a chance to buy back before he put on the bite, for twenty. And, because he'd genuinely forgotten, he was startled when Dick reminded him that he already owed him ten dollars from three weeks before. "My God," Ray said, "I clean forgot. Why the hell didn't you remind me sooner?" And then, because it was the only way out, he laughed and made a joke of it, pulled a ten out of his wallet and handed it to Dick. "Now we're all even; let's start over. Can you lend me twenty, just till Saturday?" He'd still come out ten ahead, he thought. But Dick Johnson had shaken his head. "Sorry, Ray boy, I'm short this week myself. Need all I've got, and this ten comes in handy too." And there went the ten he'd just got from Benny.

He stopped at the corner of Fourth and Main, the middle of downtown, to make up his mind where to eat. Feratti's seemed like a good bet; they put out good dinners for two-fifty—unless you ordered steak or lobster or something fancy—and he wouldn't be tempted, as he might be in some of the other good restaurants, to waste some of his drinking capacity on a cocktail or two before dining; Feratti's didn't have a liquor license. He turned on Fourth and headed for Feratti's.

And, as he walked, found himself thinking about Benny again. He never should have laughed like that at Benny. Especially now that he'd learned Benny was good for a saw-buck in an emergency once in a while. Of course maybe he was worrying about nothing; maybe Benny's feelings hadn't been hurt at all. But if he passed Benny's stand again this evening he ought to stop, buy a paper as an excuse, and see how Benny acted. If Benny was mad or had been hurt, he'd know easily and now, the same evening, would be the time to square things. And he wasn't a salesman for nothing; he could convince Benny that he hadn't been laughing at *him* but at a joke he'd just thought of, and tell Benny a joke. Some simple joke that even a moron couldn't help getting.

And then, if he could figure out a way to do it, try to talk Benny out of going to the cops to give himself up as the psychopathic killer. Not that the cops would really believe Benny, but they might keep him out of circulation for a while and maybe work him over a bit for details, until they were sure.

Because the cops couldn't eliminate Benny as readily and surely as he, Ray Fleck, could. The cops didn't know what the psycho looked like, and he did. At least enough to be positive that he didn't look even remotely like Benny.

It had been about two months ago, the night of the second murder—although he hadn't known that until the next day. It had been somewhere around ten o'clock in the evening. And it had happened in the nineteen hundred block on Eastgate. Howie Borden lived at 1912 Eastgate and Ray had agreed to pick him up around ten that evening; Howie was going to take him to a stag party at Howie's lodge, and Ray was to provide the transportation since Howie had a badly sprained right wrist and couldn't drive.

He'd got there just about ten and had parked in front of Howie's house and beeped the horn. Howie had raised a window and called out, "Be about five minutes yet. Come on in." But he'd called back that he'd wait in the car. He didn't want to go in because Howie's wife might be around, and she always made him feel uncomfortable. He felt as if she saw right through him and didn't like what she saw.

Since he knew that five minutes might easily mean fifteen or twenty, he turned out his car lights for the wait. He was sitting there staring at nothing through the windshield a few minutes later when he saw the man.

The man came through the gate in the fence in front of a house on the other side of the street and three or four houses away. Ray noticed the man at all for only two reasons. One was the fact that in an otherwise completely static vista the eye is drawn to the only moving object. The other was the fact that as the man stood there just outside the gate he looked both ways and while he did so his hands at his sides were flexing and unflexing, as though they were cramped from gripping something very tightly and for quite a while. The gesture an oarsman might make when he unclamps his hand from the oars after rowing a mile or so, or a lumberjack when he lets go his ax to rest his hands after a bout of chopping. Or that a strangler might make— But Ray Fleck didn't think of that at the time. The man went the other way and was out of sight and out of mind by the time Howie came out and got in the car.

It wasn't until late the following afternoon, when he read the mid-afternoon edition of the evening paper, that he knew he had seen the murderer leaving the scene of his second crime. The address was 1917 Eastgate, on the opposite side of the street from Howie Borden's, and about three houses away in the direction in which Fleck's car had been facing. If the address had left any doubt in his mind that the house was the one he'd seen the man leaving, the doubt was dispelled by a picture of the house's exterior that was published with the story. It showed a three-foot iron fence in front; the house the man had left had been the only house on that side of the short block that had been fenced in. And that flexing and unflexing of the hands...

Give him credit. He considered going to the police to tell them what he had seen, considered it seriously. He was home and alone at the time, as Ruth had just left for work, so he had all the time to think that he wanted. He paced the apartment for all of twenty minutes before coming to a decision. The decision was negative on three counts.

First, he couldn't give them a description that would really mean anything and he couldn't—or he was fairly sure he couldn't—identify the man if he ever saw him again. He'd seen him at a distance of about a hundred feet and in pretty dim light; the nearest street light had been behind Fleck's car, farther from the man than Fleck had been. His impression had been of a man of average height and average build—or maybe a little heavier than that. It could have been his own description, except— Except what? Thinking back, he decided that, although their weight was probably about the same, the man had been a bit narrower in the waist, a bit broader in the shoulders. But he could have been wrong even about that, the nearest to a positive point he could think of; after all he was trying to describe a vague and illusive memory, something he'd hardly noticed at the time. He thought the man had worn a dark suit and a dark hat, but he wasn't sure of those things either. The face had been a white blur in the instant it was turned toward him, before the man had turned and walked the other way.

What good could a description like that do the cops? It could fit a hundred thousand guys. It could eliminate a few, sure—teenage kids, skinny guys or fat ones, runts or six-footers. Yes, it would eliminate a few who might otherwise be suspects. Benny, for instance; Benny was well over six feet, well over two hundred pounds.

But would the cops *believe* that his impression, his memory, was as vague as all that? He doubted it. Having nothing to lose, they'd operate on the theory that he might have got a better look than he remembered, that if he saw the man again his memory might come back and let him make a positive identification.

And he knew what that meant—line-ups. They'd expect him to attend the line-up every morning for God knows how long.

Could they force him to? Maybe not, but they could be damned unpleasant about it, maybe make trouble for him, if he tried to refuse. Maybe they could even hold him, for a while anyway until a lawyer could get him out of it, as a material witness.

But even that wasn't the worst thing against taking his story, such as it was, to the police. Even if the police tried to keep it under wraps there was always a chance some damn reporter would get hold of the story and print it. Complete with his name and address. And how'd you like to have a crazy killer know who you were and think, however wrongly, that you knew him by sight and could put the finger on him the first time you saw him?

The cops would try to protect him, sure. But what if the killer was smarter than the cops? He had been, so far. And how *long* would the cops be able to keep up a twenty-four hour guard duty on him, and wouldn't it mess his personal and private life to hell and back while they did?

So Ray Fleck had sensibly kept his mouth shut about what he'd seen that night. He'd even almost forgotten about it himself; he was thinking about it this evening only because of that ridiculous would-be confession of Benny's. Crazy Benny might be, but the sex killer, no.

At Feratti's he took his favorite table. It was a small one against one side of the room but a light fixture in the wall right above it made it the best lighted table, and he needed good light to read the fine print and hieroglyphics of a Racing Form. He took his out of his pocket and unfolded it, turning first to the Aqueduct results for yesterday. He swore under his breath when he saw that Black Fox had won in the fifth and had paid ten to one for a win ticket. Black Fox was a horse he'd been following and had figured was due to win. If he'd had twenty-five bucks on the nag it would have made him more than half what he owed Amico and would have taken the pressure off. Damn Joe for having cut off his credit; otherwise he'd probably have made that bet, phoned it in.

He glanced over results of the other races but with less interest; none of them were races he'd have bet anyway. He'd handicapped some of them but he'd have had to play the favorite in each if he played at all, and he almost never played favorites. You didn't win enough money to matter if they came in and they could always fool you and run out of the money. Really long shots weren't good either. The way to cash in on handicapping is to find a horse that pays better than the real odds against it, say a horse quoted at five or six to one but with one chance out of three or four of coming in. Then was the time to get the bank roll down, when the odds were in your favor.

He heard the deferential clearing of a throat and looked up; Sam, the waiter who always served this table, was standing there with a menu in his hand. "'Scuse me, Mist' Fleck. You wanna order now? Or shall I come back when you've had more time to figger them ponies?"

"I'll order now, Sam. Won't need a menu. Bring me the Special Sirloin."

"Yes, suh, Mist' Fleck. Medjum rare, like allus. An' Ah'll tell th' chef to pick out a nice big one."

Ray Fleck frowned as the waiter ambled off. He hadn't really intended to order a steak. But it didn't matter much. He'd be able to eat it; he was always able to eat. And it was probably better at that to get a good meal under his belt while he was at it.

He killed time with his Racing Form—not that he was going to do any betting tonight and probably not tomorrow, but a horse player has to stay in touch whether he's betting or not— until Sam brought his dinner. Then he gladly put the Form back in his pocket and dived in. Just ordering a steak and waiting for it had made him hungry, and he ate heartily. And rapidly, wolfing the steak as fast as he could cut it into bites. Ruth always kidded him about how fast he ate, but he could never see any use in dawdling over food.

And then, replete, he took a cigar from his pocket, unwrapped and lighted it. He sighed with a satisfaction as he inhaled the rich smoke.

The evening stretched ahead of him, a pleasant evening now, an exciting evening. True, he had to see Joe Amico, and that would be unpleasant, and a bit embarrassing. But he could handle Joe all right, no sweat at all.

And, true, he had to spend part of the evening raising money for a poker stake, but that ought to be easy; he knew hundreds of people; he'd run into dozens of them during the course of the evening. And once he had a stake, he was going to be lucky in the game. He had more than a hunch. He felt sure of it.

He caught Sam's eye and lifted a finger, a signal for Sam to bring over the check. Sam brought it over and put it face down in front of him. But he didn't have to turn it over; he knew a sirloin steak was four bucks and this one had been well worth it. He counted out four singles from his wallet and then, the fifth one in his hand, hesitated. Sam liked to gamble. "Double or nothing on the tip, Sam?"

Sam's teeth flashed, white and black. "Sho', Mist' Fleck. How? You want flip a coin and me call it?"

Suddenly Ray Fleck had a better idea. He didn't mind Sam winning, but if he did win it would be two bucks cash tonight. And cash tonight was more important than something he could pay off the next time he ate in Feratti's. He said, "Got a better idea, Sam. I'll give you *two* tips. One of 'em's on a beetle named Birthday Boy in the fourth at Aqueduct tomorrow. Oughta pay about six to one, but I dope it he's got a better chance than that of winning. Want me to make book on him for you for a buck?"

Sam laughed. "Birthday Boy! Man, that's a real hunch bet, fo' me. Tomorra's my birthday, Mist' Fleck. Sho. An' I'm go-in' to try to put some more dough down on him aftah wuk tonight. You said fourth race, Aqueduct?"

"That's it. Say, I'm seeing my bookie tonight. Want me to put down your bet for you? Might as well save you the trouble."

"That'd be fine sur. Ah might miss the man Ah mostly bet with." Sam pulled wadded bills out of his pocket. Straightened out they proved to be a five and a half dozen ones. He handed the five to Ray Fleck. "Sho 'preciate yo puttin' this down fo' me, Mist' Fleck. Thanks muchly."

"Don't mention it, Sam. Glad to." And of course he was glad, because it put him five bucks ahead. Unless, of course, Birthday Boy won, but that was something he wouldn't have to worry about until tomorrow. Not even tomorrow, come to think of it; if the nag did come in he'd owe Sam about thirty bucks but he wouldn't have to drop into Feratti's right away to pay off. He could wait till next week, after his next pay check. Sam wouldn't come looking for him.

After Sam had left he put the money in his wallet and, while he had it open, counted what was there. He was a little surprised to find out it was exactly what he'd left home with no more and no less, twenty-eight bucks.

Then he figured, and that was right. He'd got ten from Benny but had had to give the same amount to Dick Johnson. The five he'd just got from Sam covered his taxi fare and his dinner. He'd bought the Racing Form and had paid for a couple of drinks, but he must have had enough change to cover those things.

Well, he was still even. But damn it, he'd have to keep his mind on raising more, and damn fast. By rights he should have at least a hundred to sit in on that poker game. Fifty was rock bottom; he could hardly go around with less than that. Even with fifty, he'd have to count on winning some early pots or he'd go broke before he hit his stride and got really started.

Good God, wasn't there *someone* who could and would lend him a sizable chunk of cash, say a hundred, in one chunk without his having to try to chisel it out five or ten bucks at a time?

There *had* to be. With all the friends he had…

What about Ruth? Her attitude still steamed him.

She was not only being selfish as hell, but she was being penny wise and pound foolish. If she'd only cash in that ridiculous, horribly expensive endowment policy and turn over the money to him so he'd be on his feet again, she wouldn't have to work. He could and would support her. If she'd only borrow five hundred against it, she'd take him off the spot. And damn it, wasn't anything she had half his anyway? Sure it was. This was a community property state.

Damn her, if he divorced her everything they owned would be split down the line and he'd get half of it. But he didn't have any grounds for divorce. He sometimes suspected that damned Greek she worked for of being soft on her—but he doubted that Ruth had ever encouraged him or had anything to do with him. And even if she had, how could he prove it? He couldn't afford to put private detectives on her, not now. Someday maybe. And even if he tried now and succeeded, a divorce took time. And cost money; it might even cost more than he'd get out of any property settlement.

Damn the stubborn bitch, he thought; when she gets an idea in her head....

But there must be someone besides Ruth who could help him. And who would.

Suddenly he remembered a short story he'd read once, a long time ago. He wasn't much of a reader, outside of newspapers and the Racing Form, but once—before he had met Ruth—a girl he'd been going with had given him as a present a book called *Great Short Stories of the World.* And not long after that he'd been home sick for a week with a case of bronchitis and had read most of the stories in the book and had even enjoyed some of them. One of them—he couldn't remember the title—had been by a Frenchman, Maupassant or somebody. It had been about a man who'd been in a bad financial jam. He'd needed money in a hurry and had gone to his wife, in whose name he'd put a lot of his property, and had asked her for money; she'd turned him down flat. In despair he'd gone to his mistress for help—and she'd given him back all the jewelry he'd given her, and he'd been saved.

Why not? Dolly wasn't exactly his mistress but she was the next thing to one. And while he hadn't given her any jewelry to speak of, except a wristwatch once, he'd given her, times when he'd been flush, plenty of other valuable presents. Hundreds of dollars' worth over the year and a half he'd known her. Of course she didn't love him; he knew that. But she liked him a lot and she was understanding. Wouldn't she lend him a hundred bucks if he asked her? Suddenly he felt sure that she would. Especially if he gave her a profit motive by telling her that if she lent him a hundred now he'd give her back a hundred and twenty-five in a week or two. And a hundred bucks tonight would sure be worth more than that some other time, when he was solvent again.

Sure, Dolly would do it. If not because of Cupid, then out of cupidity. Ray Fleck grinned to himself. Maybe there was something to reading great literature after all. If he hadn't read that story he might never have thought of Dolly Mason as a source of money. If only she was home, and alone, so he could see her this evening...

Well, he could find out right away. He got up and got his hat first so he could leave right after the call, and then went to the phone booth. He dialed Eastgate 6-6606, Dolly's number—and a very easy one to remember. When the phone rang a dozen times or so he frowned, realizing that it wasn't going to be answered.

Then he thought to look at his wrist watch and realized why. Dolly was out somewhere eating dinner at this time. Her apartment had a kitchen but she never kept food in it; she always ate out. Alone, if there wasn't anyone to take her out. She never cooked, either for herself or for company.

He hung up and got his dime back, then left the booth. On his way out he passed Sam turning in some money at the cashier's desk and said, "Happy birthday, Sam. Hope your hunch hits."

Sam said, "Thanks muchly, Mist' Fleck. Ah hopes we both hits it big on that pony."

7:25 P.M.

It was dark outside now, and the blackness pressed against the windowpanes of the restaurant. Funny, Ruth Fleck thought, how black that blackness looked, because if you went outside through the door the sidewalk wasn't really dark at all. It was lighted by a street lamp not far away and by the lights of the restaurant itself shining through the big front windows. But from inside it looked like a solid wall of darkness. She paused for a moment and studied her reflection in glass. It felt as see were looking at someone else, an apparition.

Things were quiet now; the early dinner rush was over. There were four people still eating at one of the tables, a couple had just come in and were studying the menu at another, but both tables were in Margie's territory. At this time of evening, with two waitresses on, Ruth had only the counter—there were three people eating at it but they had all been served—and the two tables nearest the back end of the counter. In a few minutes there'd be only one waitress on; Ruth took off from seven-thirty to eight, to eat and rest. When she came back on Margie left for the day and Ruth took care of things alone the rest of the evening. Usually she could handle things quite easily alone. Mikos' Restaurant was a family type restaurant on the main street of a suburb; its customers were people of the type who ate their dinners relatively early and business after eight wasn't too heavy. Sometimes there was a flurry between ten and eleven—people dropping in on their way home from movies—and George came on and helped her.

She looked at her customers at the counter. One was just finishing and she walked down the counter to him. "Dessert, sir?" He was a clean-looking, well-dressed young man with blue eyes and dark curly hair. He looked up at her. "Thanks, no. I'd like some more coffee, though."

And, while she was pouring it, "I beg your pardon, hope you won't think I'm fresh, but I heard the other waitress call you Ruth. May I ask the rest of your name? Mine's Will Brubaker."

Here comes a pass, Ruth thought. But she didn't really mind; it happened about once an evening and she'd probably have wondered if it hadn't happened—have wondered whether she was losing her appeal and attractiveness. Of course there was always George Mikos to convince her that she wasn't. George was a rock.

And this young man was nice, shy; he'd had to work up his courage to take the first step of asking her name. She smiled at him. "Ruth Fleck," she said. "Mrs. Ruth Fleck." She didn't embarrass him by emphasizing the *Mrs.* but it was clear enough.

"Oh," he said. "I'm sorry."

"For what? It's my fault, not yours. I keep my rings in my purse while on duty because I don't like to work with them on. So you couldn't have known I was married." She took out her pad of checks and a pencil. "I'm going back into the kitchen now to eat my own dinner. I'd better give you your check."

"Sure. Uh—shall I pay it now?"

"Oh, no. The other waitress will take care of you at the register." She smiled again, a little mischievously this time. "Her name is Margie Weber and she's single."

He grinned and said "Thanks." He should have, Ruth thought. Margie was a very cute little redhead, much prettier, Ruth thought, than she herself was. And occasionally Margie did let customers make dates with her if they were nice enough; she might well think this one was nice enough.

The clock on the wall now said seven-thirty. Ruth caught Margie's eye and pointed toward the back of the restaurant to show that she was taking off. Margie nodded.

Ruth went back into the kitchen and through it to the closet-dressing room where the waitresses put their coats and those who didn't wear their uniforms to and from work (Ruth did) changed into them. She looked into the full-length mirror on one wall and liked what she saw there. She was tall for a woman; in high heels she was only an inch shorter than Ray, who was five feet ten. But she was slender and had a nice figure. The tiny waitress cap enhanced rather than hid her golden hair. Her eyes were deep blue. The only fault she could find was in her face; it was a square, honest face, attractive but not beautiful, with high cheekbones almost like an Indian's. The mouth was perhaps a trifle too wide, but the better for that when she smiled.

Right now, though, she wasn't smiling and her face looked tired. Well, it had a right to be; she'd cleaned the house thoroughly today; quite a bit of work to undertake before coming on for an evening shift that kept her on her feet almost all the time. That and the quarrel with Ray; quarrels always left her physically as well as emotionally exhausted.

But her eyes no longer showed that she'd been crying; two hours of work had taken care of that. Her nose was a little shiny though and she powdered it lightly, turned and looked over her shoulder to make sure her slip didn't show, and then went out into the kitchen again.

Tex, the cook, was taking advantage of a hiatus in order to scrape the big range. He nodded to her. "Some nice little club steaks, Ruth. Shall I fry one for you?" She shook her head. "Thanks no, Tex. I'll just help myself to something." She took a plate and went with it to the steam table, helped herself to a stuffed bell pepper, a small helping each of beets and peas, and took it to the table in the corner. It felt good to sit down and get off her feet.

She heard George Mikos come out of his office and walk up behind her. He said, "That isn't much of a meal for a healthy wench, Ruth."

She looked up at him over her shoulder. "I'm just not hungry. I'm going to have to make myself eat this much. I guess I don't feel very well."

"Want to take the rest of the evening off? I can handle things easily. Or maybe Margie would want to get in a little overtime."

"Oh, no, George. I'm not sick. Just a little tired." She smiled up at him. "I'll get my second wind soon." She wasn't exaggerating; it happened every evening when she'd done quite a bit of housework. She'd be tired for the first few hours of the evening and then get second wind and feel fine the rest of the time.

"All right," he said. "When you're through eating don't forget you wanted to talk to me about something."

He walked away and she could tell by the sound of his footsteps that he went through the swinging doors to the front of the restaurant. She noticed for the hundredth time how lightly he walked for so big a man. She wondered if he was a good dancer and decided he probably was; most men who are light on their feet are. Ray hated dancing and she'd danced only a few times since she'd been married.

Ray took her out about once a month, on one of her evenings off, never to a show and never to dance. Even if they went to a night club where there was dancing between floor shows. Ray's idea of an evening out with her was to sit at a booth in a tavern or, if he was flush, at a table in a night club, to drink and talk. To talk, that is, if he ran into friends of his whom he could get to sit in the booth or at the table with them, as generally happened. If they were alone he was generally quiet and moody as though taking her out was a duty and he resented the loss of an evening that it entailed. And in either case they generally got home earlier than he himself would have come home had he been without her. She came away from these evenings out with Ray with a distinct emptiness that was increasingly difficult to dismiss.

She supposed she might as well admit it—to herself; her marriage with Ray had been, thus far at least, a failure. But she also had to admit that it was partly her fault; she should have known him longer—and got to know him better. She had known, of course, that he enjoyed gambling, but she had no objection in principle to gambling, as long as it was in moderation. Her father, whom she had loved deeply, had gambled all his life and had been a wonderful man. She just hadn't known Ray well enough to know that with him gambling wasn't a mild vice, as it had been with her father, but was an obsession, the most important thing in his life. He was addicted to it as some even more unfortunate people become addicted to morphine or heroin. He had neither the will nor the will power to stop, and she felt sorry for him.

She wondered sometimes if Ray realized by now that their marriage had been a worse mistake for him, in all probability, than it had been for her. His mistake had been not in marrying her in particular; she was probably as tolerant a wife as he could have found. It had been in marrying at all. He had been made to be a bachelor. (Spoiled by a doting mother? He never talked about his early life and all she knew about his parents was that they were dead, as were her own.) He wasn't made for married life, for domesticity. He didn't want a home of his own; he'd have been happier living in an uptown hotel, as he had lived before marriage, even than living in a rented flat. She wondered if he'd ever thought of their getting a divorce; he'd never mentioned one, not even late this afternoon when they'd had their worst quarrel to date. Or had that been because he still hoped that she might relent and either cash in or borrow against that policy to give him the money he wanted?

She'd finished eating and got up and put her plate, knife and fork with the dirty dishes. The kitchen clock showed her that only ten minutes of her lunch period had gone by, and George was still up front.

It was uncomfortably hot in the kitchen. The door to the alley was open and the light outside was on. She went through it and a step to one side to stand there for a breath of cool, fresh air. Well, cool air, anyway; the row of garbage cans to the other side of the door kept it from being too fresh.

There were quiet footsteps again, and then George stood beside her. He said, "You shouldn't be out here in the alley, alone."

"It's safe, George. It's right under a light and right outside the door. I'd have plenty of time to get back inside if I saw or heard anyone coming from either direction."

"I suppose so," he said. "I guess I worry too much. But did you read the editorials in both of yesterday's papers?"

"No, I didn't. Something about the—the psycho?"

"Yes, and it was something that needed to be written. In fact, the police suggested to the editors of both papers that it *be* written, and my friend, the captain in charge of homicide, talked it over with me before he made the suggestion to them. I've got a copy of one of the editorials—and the other says approximately the same thing—in my office if you'd care to read it. Or I can tell you what it says, if you'd prefer."

Ruth said, "I think I'd as soon you tell me, if you don't mind. I suppose it warns women to stay out of dark alleys."

"Among other things, yes. You see, Ruth, a criminal—whether sane or psychotic—does tend to repeat the pattern of a crime. The *modus operandi*. But unless he's a moron he'll vary the pattern if and when his *modus operandi* becomes impossible, for any reason, for him to repeat.

"And that's exactly what our psychotic killer is going to find himself up against if and when he decides to commit another crime. We don't know what kind of a gimmick he used to get his first two victims to open their doors for him, but whatever it was it's not likely to work for him again. Every woman in the city is scared and has been since the second crime, since it's looked as though he may be starting a series of such crimes."

"I see," Ruth said. "And the police think he'll try a different— uh—*modus operandi* the next time?"

"They do. He'll almost have to, to succeed. Just what he'll try, they don't know, of course. He might slug a woman on the street and drag or carry her into an alley or an areaway. He might break into her place while she's away and be there waiting for her when she comes home and lets herself in.

Those are the two main possibilities, but there are others. The point is, a woman can't consider herself safe just because she keeps the door bolted whenever her husband is out. Not that she should neglect that precaution, either. He may try his former method several times, and vary it only if he finds out that it doesn't work. You *do* have a chain bolt, don't you?"

"Not a chain bolt, just an ordinary one. I've been using it since the scare started. Ray doesn't like it much, having to wake me up to let him in when he gets home after I do, but he goes along with it."

"I hope you make sure it's Ray before you unbolt the door."

"Oh yes. And not just by recognizing his voice. We have a code. It's—"

"Don't tell me." He interrupted almost sharply. "I mean if you have a recognition code that's good, but you shouldn't tell *anybody* what it is. Ruth, you said at five-thirty there was something you wanted to talk to me about. Shall we talk here, or go into my office?"

"I guess we can go inside. I'm cooled off now."

He followed her through the kitchen and into his sanctum, leaving, as always, the door a little ajar. He motioned her to the comfortable reading chair, then turned the chair at the desk around to face her and sat down. He said, "I hope it's not bad news, Ruth. That you're thinking about leaving or anything like that."

"No, nothing like that, George. Do you know a man named Joe Amico? He's a bookie."

George frowned. "I know him slightly. And know a little about him. He's not small time but not quite big time either, somewhere in between. He operates from an apartment on Willis. I don't know whether or not he lives there too. What do you want to know about him?"

"Ray has gone in debt to him, betting, and can't pay off. About five hundred dollars, he says. He wants me to cash in or at least borrow against my insurance policy—the one I told you about—and give him the money to pay off Amico. He says if he doesn't pay Amico will have him beaten up badly, maybe even killed. I—I didn't quite believe him and I said no. But what if I'm wrong? I'd never forgive myself if something *did* happen to Ray, something bad, because I wouldn't give him the money. What do you think?"

George Mikos shook his head slowly. "It's a bluff. I don't know whether Ray was trying to bluff you or Amico was trying to bluff him, but Amico isn't going to risk everything he's got by going in for violence, over an amount like five hundred dollars.

"He's a fairly slimy character, I'd say—a half-pint who wouldn't weigh over a hundred pounds soaking wet who has an inferiority complex over his size and tries to act like a Little Caesar to make up for it—but he's also a smart operator who has a good thing and knows it. He pays protection, and gets it, but the police aren't going to let him get away with beating up people, let alone rubbing them out. Besides, he's more interested in getting his five hundred dollars than in fixing things so he can't get it."

Ruth sighed audibly with relief. But she couldn't quite believe it. "You mean Ray could just not pay him and nothing would happen?"

"Not quite that. He'd make trouble, I imagine. But not in the way of physical violence. He could get Ray marked lousy with all the other gamblers so they wouldn't have anything to do with him. He might even manage to make him lose his job; Amico has connections. But he'd do that only as a last resort—he'd much rather get his money even if he had to take it so much every week, and he couldn't very well do that if he lost Ray's job for him. No, Ruth, I don't think you have anything to worry about. Nor has your husband, except that he's going to have to get along with less spending money—or gambling money—for a while."

Ruth Fleck stood up. "Thanks, George, thanks an awful lot. I—I was horribly worried that I'd done the wrong thing, but what you told me is exactly what I hoped you'd say. Thanks a million."

"Sit down again, Ruth. It isn't eight o'clock yet, is it?"

"I'm afraid it is—almost. And I don't want to make Margie have to stay overtime. Maybe we can talk again later."

When Ruth got back up front the first thing she noticed was that the shy young man had left. Either he hadn't had a chance to talk to Margie or she had turned him down, otherwise—since she'd be getting off work so soon—he'd have waited around. There was one customer at the counter but Margie had served him and he was just starting to eat. There were parties in one of the booths and at two of the tables, but they'd been served too.

Margie came over and talked a minute and then, cold on the stroke of eight, went back to change into her street clothes. Since she was so often picked up at eight for a date Margie never wore her uniform to and from work, as Ruth did.

Ruth checked he big chromium coffee urn to make sure there was plenty in it and then went up to the cash register; there was a stool behind it where she could sit down when there was nothing for her to do. She sat down and looked out through the window, at nothing.

She did, as she had told George, feel better now, much better. Her conscience didn't bother her as to whether or not she had done the right thing in turning Ray down on the money. She'd hated the nagging thought that she might be getting him into serious trouble, sent to the hospital or even killed.

But if losing his job was the worst thing that could happen to him—well, that might be for the better. He was a good salesman and could easily get another job—selling hardware or groceries or something safe. With his weaknesses the job he had, making him spend most of his working time in taverns, was the worst job possible for him. In another job he might make less money for a while but that would be all right. Or even if he kept his present job, having gone into debt over his head from gambling might be a good thing to have happened to him. If he had to pay Joe Amico off a little at a time out of his earnings he wouldn't have much left to gamble with and might, during however long it took him, get out of the habit of gambling so heavily. That was all she asked; she didn't mind if he kept on betting on the horses if he made small bets, ones he could afford to lose.

At any rate he was past the limit of his credit now; he'd *have* to behave himself for a while. And if, after he'd worked himself out of the hole this time, he didn't straighten out—

She didn't carry through with the thought consciously, because she still did love him, at least a little, and she hated the thought of divorce. But down deep she knew it was something that would have to happen eventually, unless Ray changed—and down deep she knew that he would never change. And her insurance policy was an ace in the hole there; if he should want to contest a divorce she'd have to go to Nevada to get one—but her policy would cover even that.

George Mikos would be more than glad to finance one for her, but she'd never let him do that. Nor would she let her growing feeling for George, her knowledge of how *secure* it would be to be married to him, affect her decision. Whether or not she would stay with Ray depended solely, in all fairness, on Ray himself, whether he overcame his weakness or let it overcome him.

She wondered what he was doing now, out there in the darkness...

8:03 P.M.

Out there in the darkness—but downtown, where it wasn't dark at all—Ray Fleck was passing a tavern. It was called Chuck's Chuckhouse, although it was basically a tavern and served only cold sandwiches in the way of food, and was run by Chuck Connolly. It was the one business stop Ray really *should* make this evening; he was overdue to make a call there and Chuck always gave him a good order, including half a dozen to a dozen cases of Ten High, which he used as his bar whisky. Ray had been distracted by his financial troubles and hadn't worked very hard that afternoon. He had only a few small orders to turn in and seeing Chuck tonight would make the difference between having a good batch of orders to turn in at the office tomorrow or a poor one. Besides, if he waited too long to call Chuck might possibly change his bar whisky and order from another outfit. Losing Connolly as a customer would cut into his income appreciably. He couldn't risk that.

Just the same, tonight, he wanted to be sure the place wasn't crowded before he went in. It's customary for a liquor salesman to stand a round of drinks for the house when he walks in to get an order and Ray Fleck didn't want to get stuck for ten bucks or so for that round. True, he'd put it on the swindle sheet—and make it a little higher than it actually was—and get his money back eventually. But that wouldn't help tonight; he'd spent three bucks since his steak dinner and hadn't been able to borrow anything so he was down to twenty-five already and getting seriously worried about that stake. This seemed to be a hell of a bad night for running into people he could borrow from, and a ten-buck round would put him down to fifteen dollars. That was chicken feed—not nearly enough build on. He'd better come up with something fast.

So he walked past first, turning his head to glance in the window, but staying on the outside of the sidewalk so Chuck would be unlikely to see him.

But he was lucky; Chuck was behind the bar and there were only three men in front of it, so he turned and came back and this time went in. He could see now that there was also a couple sitting in a booth. That meant seven drinks, counting one for himself and one for Chuck, but it still wasn't too bad.

Chuck said, "Hi, stranger. Wondered if you'd deserted me." Ray said, "Hi, Chuck. Set 'em up, huh? I'm going to use your telephone a minute."

He went on past and to the phone booth at the back and dialed Dolly Mason's number for the third time this evening. There still wasn't any answer.

He came back and sat down at the bar, watched while Chuck made drinks. He made two for the people in the booth first and took them over. He said, "Compliments of Mr. Fleck there." The couple looked over and thanked him and Ray nodded to them. He didn't know any of the customers so he didn't have to talk to them; he was just as glad because he didn't feel like talking.

Damn Dolly Mason, he thought. Was she going to be out all evening, just when he needed to see her? The more he thought about it the surer he felt that Dolly was his only good chance to borrow money in any sizable chunk this evening. And also that she'd give it to him if he could connect with her. He'd ask for a hundred; surely she'd have at least half that much on hand. It made sense, that short story he'd read once; the Frenchman knew what he was talking about. A wife will turn you down when a mistress won't. A wife has got you hooked, and knows it; a mistress is more understanding. Well, he'd keep phoning every fifteen or twenty minutes until he got her.

Oh, he wasn't the only man in Dolly's life, not by a long shot. He knew that. But she liked him a lot; he didn't think it was *only* because of the presents he gave her that she was so nice to him. If it was only that, then she was really a wonderful actress; she should be in Hollywood instead of here.

Dolly was tiny, not over five feet tall, and very slightly on the plump side, a brunette with olive skin. Just the opposite of Ruth on all counts; that was probably what had attracted him to her in the first place. A man likes a change. And she was vivacious while Ruth was quiet. She liked to drink; Ruth didn't, much. She was frankly passionate whereas Ruth— well, Ruth hadn't been cold at all when they were first married but she was tending more and more to become that way. Of course she said that was his fault, but he had a hunch that wives always said that.

Connolly was making drinks for the bar now, one screwdriver and two highballs for the strangers and a highball for Ray; he'd pour his own drink last, the short straight shot he always took when someone bought him a drink.

Ray watched him, thinking how easy it would be to borrow ten or twenty bucks from Connolly, once he'd got his order. But it was the one principle he'd always stuck to—never borrow money from a customer. His one virtue, he thought sourly; let them carve it on his tombstone when he was dead: "He never borrowed money from a customer." Besides, if he ever did and if J. & B. Distributors ever found out about it he'd lose his job like a shot. A salesman always had to appear prosperous whether he was or not.

Connolly passed around the drinks; there were thanks and skoals and everybody took a sip except Connolly who downed his short straight shot at a gulp and then looked quizzically at Ray.

"Well, I guess you want an order, huh?"

"Could use one." Ray grinned at him. "And you could use some liquor by now, I'd guess. Here, let me pay for this round before I forget." He put a five on the bar and Connolly rang up three-seventy and put a dollar, a quarter and a nickel on the bar in front of Ray. Ray jittered; the bar owner didn't sound too friendly. Was he going to say he'd already given an order to someone else?

"Yep," Connolly said. "I can use some liquor. Don't stay away so long next time. I'll give you an order, but you better mark it rush so it'll be delivered tomorrow. I'm damn near out of a few things. Come on down to the other end of the bar."

He moved that way and Ray picked up his drink—but left his change where it was—and followed, walking around the three men he'd bought drinks for. On the way, now that his mind was relieved about the order, he had a sudden thought. Maybe he could leave here with more money than he'd come in with at that. Connolly played the ponies, not regularly but frequently, and they often talked about the races and traded tips or hunches. If he could talk Connolly into making up his mind about something for tomorrow, he could say he was going to see Joe Amico later, which he was, and offer to place the bet. And, of course, keep it to cover himself, as he'd done with Sam the waiter. It could be a nasty wallop if it bit, worse than Sam's bet would be, but tomorrow was another day and it was tonight he was worried about.

But he'd better get business over with first so the other matter would look casual, so when he sat down across from Connolly at the front end of the bar he took out an order blank and spread it open on the bar in front of him, took out his ball point. "Okay, Chuck," he said.

"How many Ten Highs?"

He got a good order, better than he'd expected. Ten cases of the bar whisky, a case each of gin and vodka, the equivalent of a couple of mixed cases of Scotch, rye and other brands of bourbon, and some wine. A mixed case of vermouth, half dry and half sweet, and a few odd bottles of cordials and liqueurs. It didn't take long; Connolly always knew exactly what he wanted and the exact quantities and talked almost as fast as Ray could write it down. And Ray had learned long since not to try to increase any of the orders Connolly gave him or to try to sell him anything he didn't ask for.

Connolly was just saying "That's it, Ray," when two more men walked into the bar. Again strangers to Ray; his friends seemed to be staying home in droves this evening. Connolly excused himself to serve them and Ray called after him, "On me, Chuck." That would just about kill the change out of his five and he hoped no other customers would walk in till he could get away.

He took the Racing Form from his pocket, spread it open on the bar in front of him and pretended to be studying it; that would automatically bring conversation into the right channel when Connolly came back.

It did. He was actually studying, not pretending at all, when he heard. Connolly's voice. "See anything that looks good?"

He looked up. "Sure, Chuck. Blue Belle in the fifth. That's a filly you've been following, ain't it?"

"Yeah, but she's cost me money doing it, damn her. Hasn't run in the money last five times out. Used to be a good horse, especially on a fast track, but I'm beginning to think she's had her day."

"Hell, Chuck, ten to one they've been holding her back. She was running too well for a while and it shot the hell out of the odds. Now the odds are good again and I figure she's due. Now's the time to win back, and maybe get even more than she owes you."

"Maybe you got something there. I ain't seen a Form today. Lemme see who she's running against."

Ray handed him the Form and pointed out the race so he'd not have to look for it. He said, "And Aqueduct'll be a fast track tomorrow. No rain there for two weeks and none in sight."

"Yeah," Connolly said after a minute. "I guess I'll put something down on her."

"I'll be seeing Amico soon as I leave here," Ray said casually. "Got a date with him. If you want me to save you calling him I'll put your bet down for you when I put mine."

"Might as well," Connolly said; he took his wallet out of his hip pocket and then hesitated. "Wonder whether to put ten on the nose or fifteen across the board."

An across-the-board bet, Ray thought, would get him five bucks more—and would cost him less if the horse did win. "I'm playing her across myself," he said. "Thirty bucks, ten each way. So if she even runs third I'll break even."

One thing he'd learned long ago: if you give a man a tip on a horse let him think you're betting at least as much as he is and preferably more. That way if the horse loses he blames you less, because you've lost too; you're a fellow sufferer.

This time it paid off even better than he'd expected. Connolly hesitated only a second and then took a twenty and a ten out of his wallet, handed them over. "Make mine the same way," he said. "If you can go thirty I guess I can."

"Good," Ray said. He put the bills into his wallet, holding it with the open edge toward himself so Connolly wouldn't be able to see how little had been in it before—a ten and two fives.

He looked at his wrist watch and pretended to be surprised by what he saw there. "Good God," he said. "A quarter after—and I told Amico I'd seen him at eight. I'd better run. Maybe see you later in the evening, Chuck. So long."

Outside he took a deep breath of the cool evening air and decided that he felt swell, and that his luck had turned. Thirty bucks in one crack, even if he'd had to spend five to get it. And he now had fifty—enough, if a bare minimum, to get into the big game that would *really* change his luck.

And since his luck had changed maybe he'd find Dolly home now if he called again.

He went into the drugstore on the next corner and dialed her number in the phone booth. And this time, after seven rings—a lucky number?—Dolly's voice answered, a bit breathlessly.

8:17 P.M.

Dolly Mason heard the first ring of the phone when she was in the hallway outside her apartment, returning from dinner with Mack Irby. Mack was with her and she thought she had a free evening to spend with him. She ran to the door, fished the key out of her handbag and stuck it in the lock. It jammed there for several rings of the telephone inside, till Mack said, "Let me, Doll." He reached around her and turned the key. Dolly got to the phone just as it finished the seventh ring. "Hello," she said, a bit breathlessly.

"Hi, Dolly," the phone said to her. "This is Ray. Ray Fletcher."

"Oh. Hi, Ray honey. Long time no see."

"Too long. Can I see you a while tonight? Just for a few minutes?"

"Well—maybe just for a little while. But not right away. 'Bout an hour from now, huh?"

"An hour? Can't you make it a little earlier than that, Dolly?"

"Well, maybe a little earlier." She looked at her wrist watch. "Nine o'clock? That's a little over forty minutes."

"Swell. See you at nine. Bye now, till then."

The phone clicked before Dolly could say anything more, so she cradled it.

Mack Irby, who had made himself comfortable in an overstuffed chair, looked at her with amusement. "You wouldn't of had to stall the guy, Doll," he said. "He could of come right away. Me, I chase easy. I'm on the free list."

"Damn you, Mack honey. You're not *on* the free list. You *are* the free list. And the reason I didn't tell him to come right away is I didn't want him to come right away."

Dolly didn't mind Mack kidding her about the free list, but that was because Mack was special; if anyone else had ever said anything like that, she'd have bawled the hell out of him—and meant it.

Dolly Mason was not a prostitute. She'd never taken money from a man and never would. She earned her own living, as a beauty operator. And it was a fairly good living because she owned a one-third interest in the beauty shop and shared in the profits. Her two-room apartment living room and bedroom, with a kitchenette off the first and a bath off the second—was in a good building in a good neighborhood. Despite the fact that it was fairly expensive as were her clothes and her standards of living in other directions, she had a modest balance in the bank. Her living standards would not, of course, have been quite so high if she did not accept presents some of which she used and some of which she converted into money—from a score of men, but she would still have lived comfortably. And why shouldn't she accept presents from men—for doing something she thoroughly enjoyed and would have done for free if it were not for the fact that there were men, more men than she could possibly take care of, who would gladly bring her presents for doing what she most enjoyed.

Dolly Mason had been graduated five years ago from high school in a small town a hundred miles downstate with a reputation that made it quite inadvisable for her to stay in that town. If she hadn't had sex relations with every boy in her class it hadn't been her fault, and she'd made up the deficit by having slept with quite a number of older men.

Fortunately for Dolly her father had died just a week after her graduation leaving Dolly since her mother had died years before— the sole beneficiary of a few thousand dollars in insurance. She had left town and had come to the city immediately after the funeral. She had kept her capital mostly intact by working part time while she took a beauty course, had worked two years as an operator for someone else to gain experience, and then had used what was left of the capital to buy her way into a small but profitable suburban beauty shop. The business started out slow but eventually built up a healthy clientele.

She liked any and all men, but since she had a wide choice of them she limited her friendships (as she thought of them) to ones who were reasonably young, reasonably attractive and reasonably prosperous. They had to be reasonably generous in giving her presents from time to time. And, no matter how generous they were, they had to be reasonably good in bed.

Of all men she liked Mack Irby best. She'd met him when she'd been working about a year as a beauty operator an about a year before she'd bought into the shop. She'd thought at first that she was in love with him and for a few weeks had actually eschewed promiscuity and given herself only to him. But love, to Dolly, meant only that she enjoyed sex with Mack more than with anyone else. She'd probably have married Mack during the first week or so that she'd known him if he'd asked her, but fortunately he hadn't, for she soon found out that no one man could possibly keep her happy. Not even Mack, who was more virile than most men.

So she'd gone back to promiscuity, but since Mack wasn't jealous she'd kept him as a paramour. It was about this time that she began to get the idea that, while she was going to keep her amateur standing by never accepting money, there was no reason why men—other men, not Mack, that is— shouldn't give her presents in appreciation of her favors. In fact, Mack had suggested it.

By now, only Mack was on what he called her free list. She expected presents from him only at Christmas and on her birthday. Not that she didn't get anything else at all from him. He took her to dinner several nights a week; most of her other male friends were married and afraid to take the risk of being seen with her in public. And, because of his line of work, Mack was able to do her other valuable favors. He was "in" with the cops and able to fix traffic tickets. Once he'd even managed to square a drunken driving rap which, since it was a second offense, would otherwise have carried a mandatory jail sentence. He had connections through which he could sell for her at a fair price, certainly more than she herself could have got for them, presents

which were given to her and which she didn't want to keep for
herself. And a few times when a man whom, for one reason or
another, she had dropped from her friendship roster had become
troublesome in his efforts to see her again, Mack had talked to
him and Dolly had been bothered no longer.

Mack had been a policeman once, on the vice squad. Now he
was a private detective, a lone operator who, if he was a bit on the
shyster side and did mostly divorce work, stayed nearly enough
honest to be on good terms with the police. Which made him a
very valuable friend and protector for a girl like Dolly, who,
although she did nothing seriously illegal, frequently skated on
somewhat thin ice.

"Ray," Mack was saying to her. "That's the guy who's a liquor
salesman, no? The one who brings you a case of whisky once in a
while?"

Dolly nodded. "He said he just wanted to stay a little while,
Mack honey. If he means that and doesn't change his mind
maybe I can phone you after he goes and you can come back.
Where'll you be?"

"At the office, I guess. I've got some skip-trace reports I might
as well write up. I'll be there a couple of hours. I'll go home after
that if I haven't heard from you. Should hit the pad early tonight
anyway."

"Swell," Dolly said. "Mack honey, you make us a couple
drinks while I take a quick shower. I won't be three minutes."

She walked quickly into the bedroom. She undressed quickly,
putting away the clothes she took off since she wouldn't have to
dress again this evening; she could just put on a robe when Mack
left.

She wondered if Ray would bring a case of whisky with him
tonight; that was something she was always glad to get. She
thought back and decided that he wouldn't. He'd brought a case
the last time he'd come. Dolly didn't expect her friends to bring
her a present *every* time they came to see her, if they'd brought
something fairly valuable the previous trip. Something like a
dozen pair of nylons, dollar forty-nine variety, anything that cost

no more than twenty or twenty-five dollars (and it had better not cost much less than twenty) was good only for the time it was brought. Something worth fifty was worth a couple of visits and so on up the line. Dolly didn't keep books on the presents brought her but she had a good memory and always knew who was due to bring something and who wasn't. She didn't have her rules printed and posted on the inside of her door, as rules and prices are posted inside hotel room doors, but the men who came to see her soon got the idea and could figure it the same way Dolly did. No, Ray probably wouldn't bring anything tonight and she didn't expect him to. A case of whisky, the brand he'd brought, was worth at least fifty dollars. He would have paid less, of course, since he'd have been able to get it wholesale, but Dolly didn't care about that; it was still worth at least fifty to her.

She was in the bathroom almost exactly the three minutes she'd predicted. Two minutes under the shower and one with the bath towel; she didn't dry herself too thoroughly because Mack liked her with her skin a trifle moist. And during the minute of toweling she had time to admire her body in the full length mirror on the inside of the bathroom door.

Her breasts were especially beautiful, she thought, and why shouldn't she think so when she knew they drove men crazy. Already their shell-pink, tip-tilted nipples were hardening in anticipation.

Naked and glowing she walked through the bedroom and into the living room. Mack was sitting on the sofa; two freshly made highballs, strong ones, were on the coffee table in front of it.

Naked she ran lightly across the room and sat in his lap, kissed him. His arms went around her, one of his hands cupping one of her breasts, a perfect fit.

He pulled back to break the kiss, groaned softly.

"Little bitch," he said. "How can a man enjoy a drink with you like this. The drinks will have to wait."

He picked her up and carried her into the bedroom. She laughed; this was what she'd wanted, to have to wait for her drink until afterward.

8:24 P.M.

He stood outside a living room window of the little three-room cottage looking in, watching her. By moving from one side of the window to the other he could see almost all of the room, and she, even if she looked toward the window, would not be able to see him. There was a net curtain inside the window. From the outer darkness he could see through it clearly into the lighted room, but from where she sat the curtain would be opaque. He could—except for his Need and his desperate impatience—stand here as long as he wished to make his plans and calculate his chances.

He thought they were good. The cottage was on the outskirts of town, in a neighborhood not very built up as yet. There were only a few houses in the block.

There was one almost directly across, the street but it was dark and there was no car in the carport alongside it. Obviously either no one lived there or no one was home.

The nearest house on the right was vacant and had a "For Rent" sign on it. People were home and lights were on in the nearest house to the left—but it was well over a hundred yards away and besides either a radio or television set was turned on quite loudly. He could hear it from here. Over that volume of sound so close to them would they be able to hear the sound of a scream? He didn't think so. But it was a risk he would have to decide to take—or not to take. He'd never be able to get through the window and get to her to knock her out without her having time to scream once.

The window at which he stood was at the side of the house and he could see the inside of the front door—and the chain bolt on it. Probably just about every house or apartment in town had one now. Well, the method he'd tried three times had succeeded twice but now be might as well forget about it.

The danger that was greater than a scream being overheard was in plain sight on a stand right beside the door. The telephone. Would he be able to get through the window and to her before she could get to the phone and finish dialing a number? If she got a call through—even managed to get an operator and call *help*— *he* wouldn't have time to have his way with her. But if by then he was in the room with her, if she'd seen him, he could still take a few seconds to kill her quickly, so she'd never describe or identify him, and still, he hoped, be out of the neighborhood before the police came.

It would all depend on how quickly he could pry that window up and get into the room.

He weighed the other chances against him. He'd checked the garage behind the house; the door was open and the car was gone. That meant that her husband, if she had one, was out and not in the bedroom or the kitchen. Of course the husband might return too soon, but that would be too bad for the husband unless he was a heavyweight champion boxer. He'd hate to have to interrupt himself to do it, but he could handle any ordinary unarmed man. The only difference would be that he'd be leaving two corpses behind him this time instead of one. Or three or more corpses if by any chance a child or children asleep in the bedroom. He wouldn't mind killing them at all; he hated children almost as much as he hated women.

His eyes went back to the woman. She was sitting on the sofa, her feet curled under her, reading a magazine. Well— what was he waiting for?

He took the heavy chisel out of his pocket and put its edge between the bottom of the window and the sill, then put both hands on the handle and leaned his full weight against it. It made no appreciable sound; she hadn't looked up from her magazine. But it was in as far as he could push it, and was it in far enough?

There was only one way to find out. He threw all his strength into pushing down on the handle of the chisel, and this time there was noise—but it was the noise of splintering wood and not the snapping of the window catch above. He had failed.

She looked up now, and there was fright in her face, but not panic. She didn't scream. But she ran for the telephone and started dialing.

And there was no chance of getting to her in time now, with a second try at the window. He ran to the car he had parked a quarter of a block away. Stupid, he thought; he should have found the telephone wire outside the house and snapped it. Then he'd have had time to get in while she struggled with a dead phone. Next time, if he tried this method again, he'd do that. And he'd have a hammer to use with the chisel, to drive it far enough in so the catch would cleanly snap instead of the wood splintering.

This time he was six blocks away when he heard the approaching sirens. But would one of them by any chance stop and investigate a car driving away from the address to which they'd been called? There wasn't much traffic out here, and the cops just might get that bright idea. They weren't in sight yet so he quickly parked at the curb in front of a house, turned his lights and lay down across the front seat out of sight. They wouldn't investigate an apparently empty parked car this far from their destination.

They didn't. Two of them screamed past him. No more seemed to be coming, so he started his car and drove back into town, thinking despairingly that he wouldn't dare make a third attempt tonight after two unsuccessful ones. He'd have to case and plan his next kill carefully.

For tonight, he thought, the Need would have to go unsatisfied. He'd have to settle for the poor consolation of a few drinks to calm his nerves, and then sleep.

That's what he thought. But then, he had not yet met Ray Fleck.

8:26 P.M.

Ray Fleck's reluctant footsteps stopped on the sidewalk of an apartment building on Willis Street, just on the edge of the downtown business district, and he hesitated before entering it, as a man hesitates before stepping under a cold shower.

This talk with Joe Amico was bound to be an unpleasant one. But Joe had told him to come, and before ten o'clock, and Joe was mad at him already and would be madder if he didn't show up. So he'd better get it over with.

In a way, he thought, it was lucky Dolly Mason had told him not to come before nine; that gave him time to come here—Joe's apartment was only three blocks from the drugstore from which he'd phoned Dolly—and still get to Dolly's in plenty of time. Surely Joe wouldn't want to keep him more than a few minutes. What was there to say to Joe except to reassure him that he'd pay the money as soon as he could possibly raise it?

Yes, it was far better to get the interview with Joe over with now. That way, if Dolly lent him money, even fifty dollars, he could stay with her a while, almost two hours, until time to head for the game. That way he'd at least be sure of keeping his capital intact. And he knew that if she was free she'd let him stay. For that matter, it might be just as well for him to stay with Dolly even if she couldn't or wouldn't lend him money. If he spent the time elsewhere he was at least as likely to diminish his fifty dollars as to augment it.

He entered the building and saw that the self-service elevator door was closed and that the indicator above it showed that it was at the fourth floor and going up. So he didn't wait for it but went to the door that led to the staircase instead; Joe's apartment was on the third floor and he'd rather walk two flights than wait. He just wanted to get it over with.

Going up the stairs his mind went back to Joe. Damn him, he thought, it was as much Joe's fault as his that he was in this jam; Joe should have told him how deep in the hole he was getting. He hadn't kept track and had thought he was in only for maybe a couple of hundred. Until yesterday when he'd tried to phone in a fifty dollar bet. Big Bill Monahan, who worked for Joe and who usually answered the phone at the apartment, had said, "Just a minute, Ray. Joe said he wanted to talk to you the next time you phoned." And Joe had come on. "Ray-boy, don't you realize you're in the soup for four-eighty? You'd better pay that off before you do any more betting." He'd told Joe that he'd stop in, thinking at first to ask Joe to show him the slips on the bets; from the names of the horses and the amounts he'd know whether all the bets were his or not. Maybe Joe or Big Bill had made a mistake. But after the call he'd tried to remember all the bets he could and had added them. They'd come to four hundred and ten dollars and since he was sure that he hadn't remembered all of the bets, he was willing to take Joe's word on the total. But why hadn't Joe called him on it sooner? Twice before Joe had called him on running into debt, both times when the amount involved was a couple of hundred. Both times he'd been able to raise the money within a few days. The first time he'd done it on a signature loan, but that wouldn't work again because he'd got behind on his payments and had had a fight with the loan outfit. He'd paid it off eventually but the damn company had marked him as a poor credit risk. And loan companies keep one another posted on things like that. He'd found out when he'd applied for a second loan from another outfit and had been turned down. He'd raised the money that time by putting up his car for security but that wouldn't work again either right now. He'd had his present car only six months and had made only five payments on it. It was financed over a two-year period and he still owed too much on it for him to borrow anything against it. He could probably sell it for a few hundred more than he owed on it but he needed a car to hold down his job. His mind was still stretching for ideas when he reached Joe's place.

He pressed the door buzzer and after a moment Big Bill opened the door a few inches on the chain and looked out through the opening. He said, "Hi, Ray," and then closed the door momentarily so he could take the chain off and open it wide. It was a silly system; Ray had kidded Bill about it once and he'd shrugged and said, "Boss's orders." It was still silly. Were they afraid of a raid? Amico paid for protection and got it. He had to take a raid once in a while but he was always tipped off in advance exactly when one was coming usually just before a local election. When a raid came, Amico wouldn't be there nor would there be any clients. The cops would serve the warrant on Bill Monahan or whoever was working for Amico at the time, and find and confiscate some betting slips—phony ones with fake names on them; Amico would have the real ones. Monahan would appear in court and pay a fine or, if the police wanted to make a better showing than usual, sit out a short jail sentence. Amico wouldn't even get his name in the papers, and would meanwhile be opening up in a new location, already rented in advance, and spreading the word on his new address and phone number. No raid was expected tonight or Big Bill wouldn't have let him in; clients never get caught in one.

Big Bill closed the door behind Ray and said, "Joe's laying down. Had a headache and took some aspirins."

"Maybe he's asleep," Ray said. "Maybe I better come back some other—"

"No, he wants to see you. Said if he was asleep when you came to wake him up. Just a minute."

Big Bill crossed the room—a living room furnished like any living room except for the addition of a desk with two telephones on it—opened the door of the next room and looked in. He turned back and said, "He's awake. Go on in."

Ray Fleck went in and, in case he was going to have to take a bawling out, closed the door behind him. The room was a bedroom and Joe Amico was lying on the bed but on top of the covers and fully dressed. Ray had never seen him otherwise; like many small men Joe prided himself on being dapper. Even on the hottest days of summer he always wore a suit coat over a white shirt and a necktie and the shirt was always so fresh and clean that Ray thought he must change shirts at least twice a day and possibly oftener. The bed was a big one and Joe was so small that he looked almost like a doll lying there on it.

"Hi, Ray-boy," he said. "Pull a chair around where I can see you from here. I'm gonna stay flat. This damn headache—"

It was going to be all right, Ray thought; Joe wasn't angry and wasn't going to get tough about the dough. He pulled a chair around to the side of the bed and sat down. He remembered that Joe had once mentioned sinus trouble and asked, "Sinus headache?"

"Yeah. Get 'em every once in a while, in streaks, in series like. One at the same time every day for about two weeks. They get worse each day for the first week and taper off during the second. I'm over the bump this time; this is about the tenth day."

"Can't a doctor do anything for them?"

"Naw, I been to a dozen of 'em. The pills they give me don't help any more than plain aspirin. And it ain't bad enough for an operation; I get a streak of headaches only about once a year and I'd rather stand 'em than have a—what do they call it now—sinusotomy? What are you doing about that money, Ray-boy?"

"Trying to raise it, Joe," Ray said. And then, to give himself some leeway: "Might take a few days or even a week, but I'll get it."

"What if you can't?"

"Hell, I can—somehow. I've always paid you before, haven't I?"

"Yeah. But what if you can't scare it up this time, in one chunk? I know how much you make—about how much anyway—and that's quite a piece of cash for you. Close to a month's income. I shouldn't of let it get that big but I wasn't keeping track and didn't realize how far into me you were till Bill called my attention to it yesterday."

"Sure, Joe, it's quite a piece of cash. But don't worry I'll get it. And this damn losing streak can't last forever."

"Maybe not, but one can last a hell of a lot longer than yours has. That's what I wanted to talk to you about. I think you'd better lay off any kind of gambling till you're back even again—and that'll give your luck time to turn maybe. I don't run an installment business but I'm willing, in your case, to let you pay it off by the week. Say fifty a week; that'd take you a little less than ten weeks."

Ray winced. "My God, Joe! I can't pay fifty a week—I wouldn't have enough left to live on. How about twenty-five—if I can't raise the whole thing, that is."

"Fifty might be rough on you, yeah. How about thirty- five?"

"Okay," Ray said. "Give me a week to see if I can raise the four-eighty. Then if I can't pay you at least most of it I'll start forking over thirty-five every payday. A deal?"

"A deal. All right, that's settled. Isn't anything else you wanted to tell me, is there?"

A little puzzled—what the hell was Joe getting at?—Ray said, "Nothing I can think of. Except thanks, and I'll do my best to raise the dough without having to make it in installments. Well, so long."

Crossing the living room on his way out he walked almost jauntily. It was over with, and it hadn't been half as bad as he'd expected. He had a full week to raise or win the money and even if he didn't succeed things wouldn't be too bad. At thirty-five a week it would take a hell of a long time to pay off four-eighty but it would still leave him money for small bets and as soon as he started winning he could pyramid.

Monahan went to the door with him and opened it; they said so longs and then the door closed behind him. But it opened again when he was halfway to the stairs and Monahan stepped out into the hail and said, "Come back inside, Ray. You forgot something."

Forgot something? He hadn't forgotten anything. As he walked back he was thinking of Joe's "Isn't anything else you wanted to tell me, is there?" That had been puzzling too. What went on?

He went back. Big Bill held the door open from outside, then followed him in and closed it. This time there was the sound of the chain.

Joe Amico had come out of the bedroom, and in a hurry, because for the first time Ray saw him less than completely immaculate; his straight black hair was mussed from having lain on the bed and he hadn't taken time to comb it. He was sitting on a corner of the desk, legs dangling, and he no longer looked like a doll. You could have taken him, though, for a malevolent little marionette with eyes as cold and hard as marbles.

He didn't raise his voice but it was as cold and hard as his eyes. Ray felt his throat tighten.

"How long you been making book yourself, Ray-boy." This time the "Ray-boy" didn't sound like an affectionate nickname; it sounded like a swear word.

"Wha—" Suddenly in the middle of a word Ray Fleck realized what had happened, what *must* have happened. "My God, Joe," he said. "That bet I took to place with you for Chuck Connolly—he must've phoned you to change the amount or something and said I had the money for you. I have, but *honest*, Joe, I forgot, completely forgot about it."

"How many other times have you made book yourself on dough somebody gave you to give me?"

"Never, Joe, honest to God, never." And, in fact, he'd never before done it, to speak of. A few times, not over half a dozen, he'd taken a small bet, never over two or five, to give Joe, thinking that he'd be seeing him or phoning in some bet of his own; then had decided against laying anything that day himself and hadn't bothered to phone in the peanut bet. Once one of the horses had won and he'd paid off on it, twelve-forty on a two-dollar win bet. But never until tonight had he deliberately held out a bet to raise money.

He was taking his wallet out of his pocket with a hand that he tried to keep from trembling, opening the wallet to take out the three tens Connolly had given him. But Joe was saying, "The whole thing, Ray-boy. The wallet."

His eyes had been looking down at the bills in the wallet, trying to focus on it to pick out the three bills. He looked up in surprise and that made it too late. Big Bill jerked the wallet out of his hand and tossed it to Amico, who held it in his hand, tapping a corner of it on his knee, not as yet opening it.

He said, "How many bets in here besides Connolly's?"

"None, Joe. Honest to God. I've *never*—"

"Shut up. You stink, Ray-boy. Chuck Connolly didn't call me up to change his bet; I wouldn't of even known about it if you hadn't told me. Sam Washburn called me, Sam the waiter at Feratti's. I eat there often and know him; he almost always takes a buck bet instead of a tip, and sometimes adds cash of his own.

"So he called just before you came here, said he'd got worried about his bet on Birthday Boy and wanted to change it a little. Said he gave you five besides a one tip, all on the horse's nose. Got a little doubtful about the hunch and wanted to play the six across the board. And I had a hunch about *you,* Rayboy—that you've dragged down on me before by playing bookie on your own. I decided to see if you'd give me that six bucks. I gave you every break, even asked you, God damn it, if you had anything else to tell me. Waited till you were clear out the door before I sent Bill to get you back. And what happens when I get you back? You know I've got something on you and you pop off on a deal I wouldn't of known about otherwise. And then stand there with your bare face hanging out and swear Connolly's is the *only* bet you ever dragged down." He held up the wallet.   "How many other bets from today and tonight you still got in here?"

"None, Joe Honest to God, I—"

"Shut up," Joe Amico opened the wallet and, without taking them out, checked the bills in it. "Fifty bucks. How much was Connolly's bet, and on what? Don't bother lying because I'll check with Connolly on it."

"Thirty," Ray said miserably. "Thirty across, on Blue Belle. Fifth, Aqueduct."

Amico put the wallet down on the desk beside him.   "Bill," he said, "take thirty-six out of that. Make slips on both bets —you heard 'em. Then give him his wallet and his lousy fourteen bucks change back."

Monahan went around behind the desk.

Ray said, "My God, Joe, I know this looks like I was dragging down on you on purpose, but—"

"Shut up. From now on don't say a God damn word, till I finish and ask you if you understand, and then you damn well better say yes. Just yes and nothing else.

"Somebody else taking bets in my name, dragging down on me, that's one thing—the one thing I won't stand. Don't matter if it's six bucks—that's all I knew about for sure at first—or thirty-six or a million. Or six cents, for that matter.

"We're through, Ray-boy, finished. You come around here with a grand in cash and want to lay it, I don't take it. I don't deal with chiselers.

"I made you a nice easy deal—four months I'd of took to get all that four-eighty at thirty-five bucks a week. I meant it and you could of had the deal, but at the same time I was testing you, to see if you were going to give me that lousy six bucks. I knew if you ever dragged down on me you would tonight, on account of you're behind the eight-ball."

Monahan came around from behind the desk and held out Ray's wallet to him. Ray took it and put it back into his pocket with a hand that was shaking badly. Joe Amico was saying, "Do I have to tell you that deal's off now? You got a new deal and here it is. I want that money, *all* of it, by this time tomorrow night. You got twenty-four hours to raise it. I don't care how you raise it. Sell your car. Sell your wife. Rob a bank."

"Joe, I *can't*—"

"I said shut up. Bill, if he opens that yakker of his again put a fist in it. Ray-boy, I almost *hope* you can't. Because I'll get a four-eighty kick outa what I'm going to do if you don't."

He looked at his wrist watch. "Just twenty-four hours from right now I start putting out the word that you're marked lousy, that you're a cheap crook and a welsher besides. I start with all the tavern and liquor store owners I know—and I know plenty. Chuck Connolly will be on top of the list. I tell 'em if they're friends of mine they won't deal with a rat like you. I'll ask 'em to pass the word to the other guys in their racket, the ones I don't know. And some of the boys, the ones I know best and do business with, are going to phone in your boss and complain about you, about the way you treat 'em, the way you act in their joints.

"It'll take a little while for the word to get all the way around, but you'll be lucky, Ray-boy, to make fifty bucks in commission next week or to hold your job for two weeks.

"Oh, and you'll never lay another bet, even if you ever get any money to lay. I do know every other bookie in town and they come right after the bar owners. And I know who at least some of your friends are, too, and I spread the word there. By a couple weeks from now you won't be able to sit in even a penny-ante stud game in a private house.

"Okay, that's it. Now you can talk—one word and it better be yes, and no more than that. Do you understand?"

"Yes," Ray said. Hopelessly he turned to go; nothing he could possibly say would help right now, even if he dared to say it.

"Not quite yet," Amico said. "Bill, touch him up a little. Take it easy and don't mark him. Just something to help him remember."

Ray had sense enough to know that it wouldn't do any good to fight back; he'd get hurt worse if he did. He stood still and tried to make himself limp when Big Bill's left hand grabbed a handful of the front of his coat and shirt, thinking that if he went down from whatever came first maybe they'd let it go at that.

But what came first was a pair of flat-handed slaps to the face—back of the hand to one side, palm to the other. Slaps that rocked his head, stung like hell, and made his ears ring.

Then Big Bill, still holding with his left, pulled his right hand back and drove a fist like the business end of a battering ram into the pit of Ray's stomach. The pain was so great that, as his hands went to his stomach, he tried to double over and would have except for the big hand still holding his clothes bunched in front of his chest. From somewhere miles away and through a haze of redness he heard Monahan's voice say, "Enough, Joe?" and Amico's voice say, "Yeah. Put him in a chair. Don't put him out in the hall till he can walk. We don't want him laying on our doorstep."

He was in a chair and nothing was holding him now; he could double over forward in the chair and he did. He was retching. From somewhere not quite so far away he heard Amico's voice again. "And don't let him out till you're sure he won't puke on the hall carpet, either. If he pukes in here keep him till he's able to clean it up."

He heard a door open and close; Amico had gone back into the bedroom. He heard a phone ring and then Big Bill's voice answering it and then saying, "Ten to win on Rawhide in the fourth, twenty to show on Dark Angel in the seventh. Right, Perry."

He could straighten up now, and he wasn't going to puke. His stomach still hurt like hell and his cheeks stung and his ears rang, but he thought he could stand up now. He *had* to stand up and get out of here fast. For a moment he couldn't remember why, and then it came to him. His date with Dolly. She was his only chance now, or the only one he could think of. Joe Amico had meant every word he'd said.

He raised his arm to look at his wrist watch. Yes, he could still make it in time if he was lucky in catching a taxi quickly outside. Lucky that this was Willis Street and taxis were fairly frequent. He put his hands on the arms of his chair and stood up. Not quite straight; the pain in his stomach made him bend forward a little at the waist.

"You okay?" Big Bill asked him. His voice was impersonal, neither friendly nor unfriendly

"Sure. I got to get out of here. I'm going to be late for a date if I don't leave now."

"Walk back and forth a few times. When I see you can navigate, okay."

He was a little tottery walking across the room the first time, better coming back. After a few trips he was walking almost normally, as much as it hurt him to do so.

Big Bill got up and went to the door and opened it.

"Okay, Ray. No hard feelings?"

"No," Ray said.

As he walked through Big Bill said, "Believe it or not, I pulled my punch on that poke in the gut." And then, before Ray could answer, not that there was anything *to* answer, the door closed behind him and he heard the chain slide into the slot.

No stairs this time. He went to the shaft of the self-service elevator and pushed the button. The indicator showed that it was on the top floor, but it started down. He leaned against the wall opposite the elevator door to wait for it.

Suddenly he remembered something and reached for his wallet. Amico had told Monahan to take thirty-six out, but what if Monahan hadn't put back the change? But Monahan had; the wallet held a ten and some singles. Fourteen lousy bucks.

He *had* to get money from Dolly now. And he might as well try for five hundred while he was at it—what was to lose trying? If he got that much—and he'd offer *any* kind of interest to get it—he'd stay out of the poker session and not risk losing any of it. He'd keep it intact to be *sure* of being able to pay Joe tomorrow.

But fifty or a hundred wouldn't do him any good with Joe, so if that was all he could get, running it up would be his only chance.

Dolly, Dolly, he thought; *please, Dolly. Be like the mistress of the man in the French short story.*

The elevator came and the door slid open automatically. He stepped inside.

A minute later he was at the curb, looking frantically both ways for a taxi. None was in sight and he ran, doubled over a bit because his stomach hurt, to the corner, where he'd have a better chance of flagging one.

8:47 P.M.

See now as through a defective windowpane that lets in light but distorts the images that the light bears. See now into Benny Knox as he himself sees out. See a twisted cosmos peopled by phantoms who buy newspapers as they pass and then are seen no more, except for a few who come regularly enough to become real for a while and to be remembered most of the time. Through this pane Benny sees a frightening but basically simple universe run by a good God of Vengeance when sin is done.

But first let us see him from the outside, as others see him. Benny Knox was born thirty-five years ago to a mother who died in bearing him, her firstborn. His father was a Baptist minister, a fiery fundamentalist to whom Heaven and Hell were fully as real as Earth. His father, who never remarried, raised him.

During infancy he seemed perfectly normal and not only seemed but was perfectly healthy and he was always big for his age. If during the next years, those of his preschool childhood, signs of retardation began first to show and then to multiply, his father, who after all had no standard of comparison, failed to recognize them.

The fact that he was retarded wasn't known until he was entered in the first grade of school (his father hadn't 'believed in' kindergarten; all they did there was let children play and Benjamin already knew how to play). Within a month he had been examined by a school psychologist and the Reverend Matthew Knox had been called in for conference and advised to send his son to a special school for subnormal children.

Benny had attended that school for eight years, until he was fourteen. Then the school's principal had told Benny's father: "I'm afraid we've done all we can for Benjamin. He has approximately the equivalent of a third-grade education. Perhaps a little better than that in some subjects—such as reading and arithmetic. Not so good in some others, subjects that require memorizing, such as geography or spelling.

"Socially, the picture is neither too good nor too bad. He gets along reasonably well with people, especially his contemporaries, but only when circumstances force him to. He greatly prefers solitary occupations and activities. He seems to daydream; whether or not that will decrease or increase as he grows older, only time will tell.

"Morally—well, he's almost too good. It's obvious that he had very strong religious training at home and is—well, almost too literally convinced of everything he was taught."

The Reverend Matthew Knox had frowned slightly. "What he was taught at home *was* literally true," he had said.

"Of course. But, unless tempered with reason, some of the teachings of Christianity are—ah—hardly survival characteristics in our society. Or in any society for that matter. Generosity is a virtue, for example, but it must be practiced with moderation. Recently I happened to learn of a boy having come to school without his lunch. Not, mind you, because his parents are poor; they aren't. Just because he forgot it. Benjamin gave the boy his lunch and went hungry that day. When I learned of it I talked to him and explained that while it would have been a good thing for him to share his lunch with the boy he should not simply have given it away and gone hungry himself. There have been other such instances but that's the most recent one."

Benny's father had nodded thoughtfully. "I'll talk to him about it," he said. As a matter of fact, he already had, a great many times. Benny simply couldn't keep such things as baseball gloves, roller skates or kite reels, and when something was gone it was always because he had given it to a poor boy who didn't have one. Several times, when Benny knew the name of the poor boy and where he lived, the Reverend Knox had gone and got the article back; never had he encountered any poverty more real than his own. He had finally solved the problem—and without crossing Benny's desire to give to the poor—by issuing and occasionally repeating a flat order to the effect that before he gave anything of his to a poor boy he should bring the boy home with him; he would then talk to the boy and decide whether or not the boy was really poor and needed the article in question worse than Benny did. With rare exceptions, when Benny had forgotten, this had worked. Apparently none of the boys who had been taking advantage of Benny had wanted to face an inquisition at Benny's home first. But apparently Benny had not known that this edict had extended to school.

"And there is one other thing," the principal was saying, "that troubles me about Benjamin. I must say that it troubles me *much* more than his indiscriminate generosity—for I believe you can train him out of that without too much difficulty. He has a tendency to confess to having done things he did not do. His teacher tells me that several times when some prank or bit of minor vandalism has been committed she has talked to the class about it and then asked whoever was guilty of it to raise his hand; each time Benjamin's hand went up. And each time some minor punishment was meted out to him for what she believed he had done. Then one day the prank in question happened to be one she knew positively Benny could not have done, and he still raised his hand. It was a caricature of the teacher drawn on the blackboard during lunch hour and it was rather well done for a child's drawing; Benny is very poor at drawing. The teacher sent Benjamin to me to have a talk.

"His answers to me were vague and confusing. I honestly don't know whether he knew he was innocent and had some compulsive reason for offering himself as a scapegoat—perhaps guilt feelings about something else he harbored—or whether he really thought, once the question was put to him, that he had really done it."

The Reverend Knox was troubled; this was something new to him. True, whenever he had asked Benny whether or not he had committed some certain dereliction, the answer had almost always been affirmative, but he had never questioned the boy unless he was already reasonably sure Benny was guilty, so the affirmation had never been a surprise. He asked, "Could Benjamin have been with the boy who made the drawing—aided and abetted him, as it were—and thus felt that he shared the guilt and have raised his hand for that reason?"

"No. Once the teacher seriously considered drawing styles, the identity of the culprit became obvious; only one boy in the class could have done it. Once the question was put to him directly he confessed—as a matter of fact he was justifiably a little proud of the drawing—and admitted that another boy had been with him but it wasn't Benjamin. Benjamin hadn't even known of the drawing."

"I'll have a talk with him," Benny's father had said.

And he'd had a number of talks with him during the first year or two Benny was out of school. He'd made a number of tests, too. For example, if he himself should accidentally break a drinking glass in the kitchen, later he'd show Benny the broken glass and ask if he had done it. All too often, for a while, Benny would admit guilt. This always led to another and longer talk, and finally he felt sure that he had cured Benny of this fault—and he had, for a long time. Like the principal, he had never been able to decide whether Benny had deliberately made a false confession to court punishment or whether he really thought, when asked, that he had committed the offense in question.

He had given thought, too, to Benny's being able to make a living for himself in the world. At first, since Benny was too young for a full-time job, he had bought him a newspaper route. After a few mistakes, Benny had done all right on it. It was teaching Benny responsibility, he thought, and the five or six dollars a week it brought in helped out immeasurably. After a while the only help he needed was to be reminded once a month when it was time to make his collections.

When Benny was sixteen and already bigger than most men his father decided that it was time to help him find a niche in the world in the way of a full-time job. The good minister was himself in failing health and beginning to realize that by the time of his own death Benny needs must have not only a means of earning a full livelihood but a way of living alone without constant parental care and advice. The only alternative would be, after his own death, for Benny to be institutionalized and become a public charge. This was to be avoided if at all possible. Over the course of the next two years he found Benny a variety of jobs—in vain. Benny could handle almost any of them, with constant supervision, but no employer could afford an employee whom he had to watch all the time. Even at manual labor jobs, although he was plenty husky enough to handle them, Benny managed to get into trouble. Set him to digging a ditch and he would dig it into the next county unless you were there to stop him.

When Benny was eighteen and had never held a full-time job longer than a few weeks, and few that long, the Reverend Knox learned that he had only about six months to live. Fortunately, at about the same time, he chanced to learn that an elderly man who for many years made a living running a newspaper stand on a busy downtown street corner was about to retire and wanted to sell his business. Newspapers were the only thing Benny had ever got along with; if he could run a newspaper route maybe he could sell newspapers over a counter. In some ways the latter was even simpler. Every transaction was a simple cash deal instead of a more complicated monthly collection. Knox had a long talk with the retiring vendor, and bought the concession. The seller stayed on for a few days to show Benny what ropes there were. Knox saw the circulation managers of the two newspapers Benny would handle and the manager of the distribution agency that supplied him with the items he would sell; with each of them he arranged to have Benny's bills sent to the parsonage. There was nothing to it, and Benny got along fine from the start. Each evening he brought home his receipts for the day and turned them over to his father, who took care of paying his bills and managed his money for him, starting him out each day with the amount and variety of change he'd need to start business at the stand.

There remained only one problem to solve before he could die, and Knox had had its solution in mind for a long time; he had waited only until he was sure his son could earn a living. A Mrs.

Saddler, a widow and a good woman, was a member of his congregation and she ran a boarding house within walking distance of downtown. He went to see her and made arrangements for Benny to room and board with her, and for her, for a small but adequate percentage of Benny's earnings, to take over the management of his affairs.

That, too, had worked out. Each night he brought his money home to her, as he had to his father. She managed it for him, took out what she had coming for room and board, gave him an allowance of spending money—which went for candy and ice cream sodas, his only dissipation—bought clothes for him when he needed any, and put the surplus in the bank, part of it in a special checking account against which she drew for his business expenses, the rest in a savings account in his name—but which she reminded him of only when some extra expense or minor emergency necessitated his help in drawing some of it out.

This accomplished, the Reverend Knox had quit fighting the Reaper. He had given up his ministry and his parsonage, had gone to a hospital and died. Benny hovered over his father's bed for an hour, clutching his crumpled beanie cap, thinking he would wake up in just one more minute. He was eventually sent away by the nurse, and he crept down the stairs, alone.

And all had gone well for fifteen years, until Benny Knox was thirty-three. On the surface anyway; Mrs. Saddler sometimes wasn't sure what went on down inside of Benny when occasionally he had dark, unhappy, brooding spells; she wasn't able to get him to talk about them although ordinarily he prattled to her freely about anything and everything. And nothing had ever come or the spells; they'd always worn off.

Until suddenly at the height of one of them Benny, she subsequently learned, had gone to the police station one morning and had confessed to having committed a murder that had been much in the newspapers for two weeks. It had been, according to how one might look at it, a bad time or a good time for him to have confessed to that particular crime; the police had just appre-hended the real killer only an hour before; the news had not yet hit the papers or Benny would have read about it. Benny did read the newspapers during dull periods at the newsstand—the parts of them that he was able to understand and make sense of, which included crime stories and the comic page and not much else.

The police knew who Benny was and what he was; after fifteen years his downtown newsstand was a landmark and just about everyone in town knew him by sight. Many policemen knew him well enough to stop and talk a moment when they were passing his stand. So they brushed Benny off gently. They asked for his wallet and looked at the identification in it to see if it had an "in case of accident or illness notify" card with a name and address and it did. They phoned Mrs. Saddler and, after talking to her long enough to establish her relationship with Benny, they explained to her what had happened and asked her to come in and talk with them, after which she could take Benny back home with her. Which she did. And she talked to him until he was finally convinced that he had just imagined what he had tried to tell the police. Or perhaps he was not completely convinced until he read an afternoon paper with the story of the capture and confession of the real killer. Along with many people with higher I.Q.'s than his, Benny believed implicitly everything he read in print.

The next time Benny Knox confessed to a crime he did not commit, again a murder, was two years later—a year ago, when Benny was thirty-four. That time he did not get off so lightly, for several good reasons. The crime was not yet solved, and it had been a wanton, purposeless killing that bore all the earmarks of having been committed by a mentally deranged person. A few days later it turned out to have been committed by a pair of teenage heroin addicts, but until then Benny had rather a rough time of it. His story was hard to disprove; it made sense insofar as it covered all the facts that had appeared in the papers. Only one thing saved him from being actually charged with the crime and which would have been very bad for business at the newsstand, even though he would subsequently have been cleared. Some people would still have been afraid of him. The thing that had saved Benny had been his choice of a weapon. The news stories had said only that the man had been beaten to death with a blunt, heavy weapon. After the autopsy the police knew that the weapon had been a section of rusty pipe; not only did some of the wounds clearly indicate its diameter but tiny fragments of rust had been found embedded in the victim's skull. But they had not given this particular bit of information to the newspapers, and Benny's imagination had supplied him with a baseball bat as the blunt heavy weapon he had used. Moreover, he was unable to remember where he had obtained it or what he had done with it afterward.

The police, that time, were not so ready and willing to release Benny Knox. He'd given them a hard time and caused them a lot of work. For a while they'd seriously considered charging him despite the one discrepancy in his story. The rest of it made sense and could have been true. Further, they were convinced that he was, or at least had been, sincere in thinking he had committed the crime. That made him a psychopath, and it could be that he was a potentially dangerous one. If he could imagine himself to have committed a crime possibly someday he might really commit one.

They held him while Dr. Kranz, an alienist who was a friend of the police commissioner's and who usually advised the police on borderline cases like Benny's, talked to him twice and also had a long talk with Mrs. Saddler, who knew more about Benny's background and history than anyone else. Dr. Kranz saved Benny.

"Benny Knox," he wrote in his informal report to the commissioner, "seems to have a mental age of about eight. While it is true that many adults with that mental age find themselves unable to adjust to the world and to earn their own way in it, thereby requiring institutionalization, others do make the adjustment, especially ones who still have parents or other mentors to guide and help them.

"Mrs. Saddler stands *in loco parentis* to Knox, and she is a very sane and sensible woman. With her help, he does all right. Of course she is about twenty years older than he (that is my guess; I did not ask her age) and it is statistically probable that she will predecease him, but even this may not lead to his becoming a public charge. Mrs. Saddler is aware of the problem and has in mind solving it when the time comes, in other words, if and when she finds herself getting too old to run her boarding house any longer. She knows other rooming and boarding house keepers, some younger than herself, and believes she will have no difficulty in finding one willing to take over Benny. She says he is pleasant, tractable and easy to get along with, and his earnings are sufficient that he will represent a profit and not a burden to whoever takes care of him. The biggest problem, in fact, will be to find someone sufficiently honest not to make too much of a profit on him.

"So much for his adjustment to society despite his sub-abnormality and now to what you've been waiting for me to discuss, his abnormality, his fantasy of believing that he has committed crimes of which he is innocent and wishing to be punished for them. From what I can learn he seems to have been a wonderfully 'good' boy and probably did nothing that, even in his own mind, merited the punishment he now seeks. I would say that his guilt feelings were given to him by his father. His father—who raised Benny alone after his mother died in childbirth—was a fiery fundamentalist minister. He taught his son what he himself believed—a good but vengeful God, original sin, a very literal brimstone Hell, eternal damnation for the sinner. These are very heady and frightening doctrines even for a person of normal mentality.

"He feels himself guilty of unnamable sins and since he cannot name them—and thereby obtain punishment and through punishment forgiveness—he builds the fantasy of having committed a real sin, one for which he *can* be punished. A nameable real sin becomes surrogate for an unnamable one.

"The prognosis? Incurable. He may 'grow out of it' or its symptoms may become worse or at any rate more frequent. It's difficult to tell in these cases. So much of it is environmental.

"Does this mean he should be put in an institution? I personally do not think so. He will probably again—and possibly again and again—become a mild thorn in your side by confessing to other crimes. As a matter of police routine you'll have to check his story out, and thereby run into a little extra work and expense. But—at his present rate of two years having elapsed between his last confession and his current one—the cost of this slight amount of police work once in a while will be a minute fraction of the cost to society of institutionalizing him and supporting him for the rest of his life. So my recommendation is that you give society a break by letting Benny support himself as long as he can.

"I don't think there's any chance of his becoming dangerously insane. I can't guarantee that, of course—but neither can I guarantee it in your case or mine. And I can say for him what I can say for you or me: at present none of the three of us shows signs or inclination toward any dangerous aberration.

"I do suggest one precaution, however. Any time he again comes in with a confession, whether or not it's one you can immediately rule out without investigation, hold him until I can talk to him again and determine whether his degree and kind of mental disturbance is at that time such that I might want to change my recommendation."

That had been a year ago. Now Benny Knox was disturbed again. Not suddenly, not just tonight; his realization that he was the man who had murdered the two women, the man the police were looking for, had come to him gradually over the past week, At first he hadn't been sure, he couldn't really remember. But that wasn't surprising; from time to time there were so many things that he couldn't remember. Even now he couldn't remember *why* he had killed them—it must have been just because he was bad, evil. People were born evil and only through God and Jesus could they become good and even then before they could get into Heaven they must confess to the evil things they had done and be punished before they could be forgiven.

He closed his eyes and had a mental picture of his father and his father was holding out a hand to him and saying, "You've done wrong, Benjamin. Confess and let them punish you so you can be forgiven, or I'll never see you again. You'll go to hell and burn forever." His father's face was really his father's face, for there was a picture of his father's face on Benny's bureau and he saw it every day and couldn't forget what his father had looked like. But his father's body was clad in shimmering robes and seated on a throne. Benny often got his father in Heaven and his Heavenly Father mixed up and was as likely to pray to one as to the other.

He said, "Yes, Father, I will," aloud and opened his eyes. They fell upon his hands lying in front of him on a pile of newspapers. Big, strong hands. Strangler's hands. Hands that could kill easily, and had killed.

Footsteps approached and stopped, and he looked up, Officer Hoff stood there, grinning down at him. "Hi, Benny. Will you take your big paws off that pile of papers so I can take one?"

Benny lifted his hands and dropped them in his lap, out of sight, and Officer Hoff took one of the papers and put it under his arm. He didn't put down a dime, but Benny hadn't expected him to; policemen didn't have to pay for papers. He didn't know why not, but the man from whom his father had bought the newsstand had explained to him that policemen didn't have to pay for little things like newspapers. It was part of the cost of doing business, he'd explained, whatever that meant. You didn't charge policemen for their papers and then they liked you and helped you if you needed help. Well, he needed help now. Maybe Officer Hoff would want to arrest him right now. Officer Hoff was a nice man.

He said, "Mr. Hoff, I killed them two women. You want to arrest me? Or should I walk around to the station myself?"

Officer Hoff had quit grinning. He shook his head sadly. "Not again, Benny. You didn't—"

"I really did, Mr. Hoff. I—choked them to death." Benny held up his hands, the evidence.

Officer Hoff shook his head again. "Well—I'll radio in from the car. Maybe they'll want me to bring you in. I'll see. We're pretty busy tonight."

He walked downstreet to the curb where the squad car was waiting, another officer at the wheel. He got into the squad car. Benny was afraid at first that they'd drive off, and then he saw that the squad car wasn't moving. And after a couple of minutes Officer Hoff got out of it and came back.

He said, "No, they don't want us to bring you in. Lieutenant Burton—you know him? Red hair?"

Benny hadn't known the name but when Officer Hoff said, "Red hair," he remembered he'd talked a lot with a policeman with red hair, down at the station. He couldn't remember what they'd talked about, but he remembered the hair. He nodded.

"Well, he wants to see you. But there isn't any hurry. You can go ahead and sell the rest of your papers, no use their going to waste. Then you go to the station and he'll see you."

Benny nodded again. "All right, I'll go round."

"Be sure you do, and don't forget." He shook his head a third time. "Benny, you didn't kill them dames—we checked you out on it, long ago. You and a lot of other people. But just the same don't you forget to go to the station. If you don't go there right after you quit we'll have to come to the rooming house to get you."

"I won't forget, Mr. Hoff. I'll go there."

Benny sadly watched Officer Hoff get back into the squad car and watched the squad car drive off. Officer Hoff hadn't believed him either. But the policeman with the red hair would believe him, when Benny told him all about it.

9:00 P.M.

A clock somewhere was striking nine as Ray Fleck got out of the taxi in front of Doily Mason's apartment, and he knew that he was on time. He'd had trouble finding a cab and had thought he was going to be late—not that a few minutes late would have mattered but if he was very late Dolly would be annoyed; Dolly got annoyed easily if you were late for a date with her. Then just at the right moment a cab had pulled in to the curb right near him to discharge passengers, and he'd caught it.

A turn in his luck? God, he hoped so. *Everything* had been going wrong today and tonight, up till then. What had got into him to pop off about Connolly's thirty-dollar bet when it had been Sam's that Amico had been talking about! A lousy six bucks, and he *had* forgotten about it by then. Connolly's thirty had been the one on his mind. Hell, he thought disgustedly, he really couldn't blame Amico for not believing that he'd not been covering bets and dragging down right along, when he'd come up with a boner like that.

But Jesus, did Joe have to get so tough about it? Twenty four hours to raise four hundred and eighty bucks, or else. His face was still sore from the two flat-handed slaps Monahan had given him and his stomach still ached from the blow there. But those things would pass, the pain of them and the humiliation of them. But if he lost his job he was sunk, really sunk. If he lost his job the way Joe would make him lose it, under a cloud with the J. & B. Distributors and on the outs with most of his customers to boot, he'd never get a reference and never get another job, here or anywhere else, selling liquor.

Many people thought Ray Fleck was a good all-around salesman who could do well selling almost anything to almost anybody, but Ray knew better; he'd tried. His first foray into selling had been just after he'd quit high school about three fourths of the way through his senior year—he was failing in several subjects and wasn't going to be graduated anyway—and it had been a try at selling brushes door to door. He'd hated it, especially the long hours the company had expected him to work, and he'd stuck it out less than a week, during which time he'd earned seven dollars and some odd cents. He'd tried to stay home and loaf around for a while but finally became fed up with his father calling him a no-good and with not having any spending money, and he started to look for work again. During the next seven years he held a lot of jobs but none of them for very long. All in all he worked about half of the time, but he got by because his father, a certified public accountant, had a fairly good income and, after a while gave up trying to collect anything from his son in the way of room and board, so all the money Ray did make went for clothes and entertainment.

The jobs he held were many and varied. Soda jerk, counterman, assistant shipping clerk, driver of a delivery truck, what have you. He never held any job longer than a few months; half of them he quit because the work was too hard or too boring; he was fired from the rest for a variety of reasons, usually for goofing off. Once, in a bad period, he was fired for dipping into a till but luckily the employer didn't prosecute so he didn't have a police record because of it. The job he had held longest, and had most hated, during that period had been with the army when he had been drafted at twenty. And he had held that job only five months instead of the usual period. He had suddenly developed a violent allergy to wool, and since the army wasn't geared to provide special uniforms and bedding for him, it had the choice of discharging him or letting him ride out his hitch in the infirmary. It discharged him. The allergy had gradually diminished; by now he could wear wool suits except in very hot weather, but in cold weather he still used quilts or comforters instead of blankets.

Several of his jobs during that period had been selling jobs; he'd tried insurance, automobiles, hardware, and a few other things. But he hadn't lasted at those jobs as long as at others. He could turn on a pleasing personality and could make people like him, but he lacked the perseverance and determination necessary to succeed at selling, which is a lot tougher job than most people think.

Until at the end of the seven years he found himself and found the one job he both liked and could do well at. It was time that he found it, for his parents had just died, his mother only a month before his father, and free room and board were out; he *had* to keep a job if he wanted to eat regularly.

And the job he had finally found was a natural for him. He liked hanging out in taverns. He liked to be able to buy rounds of drinks and being able, within reason, to put them on an expense account. He liked the hours. The only part of the job that he considered work was the calls he had to make at liquor stores and he was willing to do that chore for the sake of the rest of the job. He liked drinking and he had an excellent capacity for holding his drinks. The job brought him into contact with others who, like himself, loved gambling and enjoyed talking horse racing, dog racing, the odds on a pennant race or matching coins for drinks. Best of all, the job let him make money—and make it doing what came naturally.

And now he was going to lose that wonderful job, unless he could raise four hundred and eighty bucks in twenty-four hours. Joe Amico had meant every word of what he'd said, and Joe could make his threats good, too. He wouldn't last a week in his job if Joe started spreading the word around. He *had* to raise that money now; it was a matter of desperate necessity.

He paid off the taxi, and that left him thirteen dollars, thirteen lousy dollars.

Dolly, he thought, don't fail me now! He'd already decided, in the taxi, not to start off by asking for any special amount; he'd just tell her he was in a desperate jam and needed every cent he could possibly get. Maybe she'd come up with five hundred and take him off the hook completely. If that happened, he wouldn't risk the poker game at all; he'd make sure of having the dough for Amico, to save his job. That came ahead of everything else, now.

Of course she probably wouldn't have five hundred in cash at the apartment, that would be too much to hope for, but a check would be all right; he'd have all day tomorrow to cash it. How much could he offer her for five hundred? To pay her back six hundred within two weeks? That ought to be enough to tempt her, but hell, he could go even higher if he had to. After all, he hadn't given her his right name so she couldn't locate him to heckle him. Not that he wouldn't pay her back as soon as he could—if she was reasonable, like wanting six for five. If he had to promise her anything extortionate, like a thousand for five hundred, then she could whistle for it and it would serve her right for being greedy. He hurried up the two flights of stairs and along the corridor, knocked on Dolly's door.

She opened it, first on the chain, and then when she saw who it was she said, "Hi, Ray honey. Just a sec," and closed the door a moment to slide off the chain and open it wide.

He went in and she stepped aside and then closed the door behind him. The chain went on again. Few women were taking chances these days, even if a man was with them.

Dolly Mason, he saw, was practically ready for action. Her otherwise bare little feet were in mules and she wore a thin silk kimono, brilliant red and stitched with gold thread, with obviously nothing at all—except Dolly—underneath it. But he was too desperately worried to be interested. Business came first, right now. Of course if he got enough money from her to end his worries for tonight, then he could relax and romp.

"Dolly," he blurted, "I'm in a jam, a hell of a jam. Life or death, almost. I need to borrow some money—just for a week or so. Have you got any?"

She took a short step back from him; she'd been going toward him to put her arms around him as she always did when he came in. "Honey, *I* haven't got any money. Where did you get a wild idea like that?" She looked toward a handbag lying on an end table by the sofa. "I've got just eight dollars—and I can't spare any of that because it's got to last me till payday, three days. Look, I'll show you if you don't believe me."

She started toward the handbag but he said, "Never mind, I believe you. I didn't mean that kind of money anyway. And cash doesn't matter. A check will do because I can cash it tomorrow and that'll be in time, because tomorrow night's my deadline. And you'll make money on it—not lose. If you can lend me five hundred I'll give you back six, in two weeks. That's how God damn important it—"

Suddenly she was laughing. Not a cruel laugh, but an amused one. "Ray honey, I haven't *got* a bank account, not even a savings account, let alone a checking one. I'm sorry if you're in trouble, but what made you think *I* had any money? Honest, I haven't. I'm sorry, dear. It's not all that bad, is it?"

Ray Fleck took a step backward and dropped onto the sofa, put his elbows on his knees and his face into his hands. He was beat. He hadn't realized until this moment how much he'd been counting on Dolly—and how ridiculous it had been for him to have done so. He didn't know whether or not Dolly was lying about not having a bank account, but he knew, and for sure, that even if she had she wasn't going to lend him any money. Not even fifty bucks that he might manage to run "up in the poker game, let alone the five hundred that it would take to bail him out of trouble. She didn't trust him that much and it wouldn't do any good to plead, to offer her a thousand back instead of six hundred. Even if she had a checking account, she'd never admit now that she'd been lying and write him a check against it.

"Ray honey, I'm sorry. Honest."

He took his hands away from his face, stared at her dully. "It's all right, Dolly. I shouldn't have—" He shook his head slowly. He'd started to say that he'd been a damn fool to expect anything but this, but there wasn't any point in finishing the sentence. The only thing to do now was to get going, go some place where he could think, and try to figure something out. He knew there wasn't an earthly chance that he could raise the four eighty tonight, but if he didn't waste time he might still build back his stake enough to let him sit in tonight's game. His luck *had* to change sometime.

"Ray, you do look beat," Dolly said. "Would a drink help? Let me make you a drink."

He started to say no, and then nodded instead. He really did need a drink now, and it seemed like ages since he'd had one. It has been at Connolly's, before that horrible scene at Amico's. "Sure," he said. "Make it a strong one, huh?"

"One strong drink coming up," Dolly said. She went around the screen that hid the kitchenette. He heard her taking down glasses from the little cupboard over the sink.

What an ass he'd been to remember that short story about the mistress who had given her—

Jewelry? Dolly had jewelry. He didn't know how much of it or how valuable it was, but it could be worth plenty. Not that she'd give or lend it to him, of course, but he knew where she kept it, or some of it. It was in a little hand-tooled leather box on top of the dresser in the bedroom. He'd never seen down inside it but he'd seen her open it and put jewelry into it. The last time he'd been here she'd been wearing long dangling earrings with green stones—emeralds?—and she'd taken them off the last thing and put them into the box before she'd thrown herself face down on the bed and rolled over into his waiting arms.

The jewelry in that little box might be worth plenty. Did he dare? There wouldn't be time now, even though the bedroom door stood ajar; it was clear across the living room from him and she'd surely hear him moving if he tried to go there. He'd have to go to bed with her to get a chance at the box, but it would be easy then; she always went to the bathroom for a minute or two immediately after.

Did he dare? Why not? He'd taken chances before, although never quite in this way, but then he'd never been in this bad a fix before either. Besides, it wouldn't really be stealing; it would be borrowing without telling Dolly about it. He'd make it up to her someday, when he was solvent again. If he couldn't get her back the same jewelry he could get her other stuff like it.

Thank *God* he hadn't given her his right name. Fletcher instead of Fleck was a little close for comfort, but all she knew about him outside of his right first name was that he was a liquor salesman. But there were a lot of liquor salesmen in the city—and the police wouldn't *know* that he'd given her his right first name, since they could find out quickly enough that he hadn't given a right last one.

Dolly came back with two drinks, both dark enough to show that she'd really made them strong.

He took the drink she held out to him and downed half of it at a gulp. It was strong enough to burn on the way down and it did help, it did make him feel better.

Dolly sat down on the sofa beside him, not pulling the kimono closed, and snuggled up against him. "Ray, honey," she said, "there's something might make you feel even better than a drink."

"A sure cure for everything?" he asked. "Maybe, Dolly. Maybe it would help. But I got to think a minute first, get something clear in my mind."

He put his free arm around her, but made no move otherwise. He didn't want to take her to bed unless he was going to take the gamble of emptying that jewel box, and if he made a pass or even kissed her he'd be committing himself. Besides, he knew that if he could get aroused, and let himself, he wouldn't have the will power not to follow through, no matter what he decided about the jewels.

But he had to decide quickly. Was the risk too great? Hell, he couldn't deny there *was* a risk—why had he told Dolly what his job was? If he'd kept that under his hat too, it would be safe as houses. But that would be pretty much of a lead, if the police really worked on it, and there was no reason why Dolly shouldn't and wouldn't report it to the police. Of course if she didn't miss it for several days she couldn't be sure who had taken it, but that was too much to hope for. Probably she wouldn't miss it tonight but probably when she dressed for work in the morning she'd go to the box for some piece of jewelry, costume or real, and that would be it. But it would still take the cops a while to get to him and if he could get rid of the stuff first—and he thought he knew where and how to do that—there'd be no proof. It would be just his word against hers and his reputation was at least as good as hers—hell, he had friends on the force who would vouch for him. Maybe his reputation was better; he'd never been in cop trouble, and maybe Dolly had. And—

He thought of the trouble he'd be in if he didn't raise the money for Amico, and suddenly made up his mind. He'd take the gamble. That is, if he *could.*

He took another slug of his drink and then put it down on the end table and leaned over and kissed Dolly. Her lips parted moistly, but nothing happened—to him, that is. Then his hand found one of her breasts and squeezed gently before he bent down and kissed the firm erect nipple of the other one and ran his tongue around it. He felt something stir in his loins and knew that everything was going to be all right. He wasn't worried or scared enough to disgrace himself in bed.

As a matter of fact, everything was better than all right. He found that the excitement of the risk he was going to take added to rather than took from his sexual excitement. It didn't last long but while it lasted it was wonderful; Dolly seemed to think so too.

And when she scampered into the bathroom afterward he walked quickly to the dresser and emptied the tooled leather box into his hand, walked back to the bed and put pieces of jewelry into the left pocket of his trousers. He'd hardly glanced at it, except to see that there were about a dozen pieces and that they included the earrings with the green stones that might be emeralds and that there was also a diamond ring and a wedding ring. The jewelry felt heavy in his pocket and he hoped it didn't show.

He was adjusting the trousers when Dolly came out of the bathroom. He didn't have to pretend to be in a hurry; he was. He told her he had an important business appointment and was late for it already and, left the moment he'd finished dressing.

When the chain slid home behind him he breathed a deep sigh of relief. He'd got away with it, thus far. And just maybe the whole answer to his problem was in his left trouser pocket. He'd soon know.

9:32 P.M.

Mack Irby stopped his two-finger typing and leaned back in the creaky swivel chair to light himself a cigarette. This was the only part of his job that he really hated, making reports. He'd rather tail a wife for her husband or a husband twelve hours straight than spend the half hour writing up a report on the activities of the suspected spouse. Whenever possible he talked a client into settling for verbal reports, but it wasn't always possible to get a client to agree to that. Some of them insisted on having words on paper for their money.

His dream was to have enough men under him so he could afford a stenographer-bookkeeper to take down the reports as dictation—he wouldn't mind talking them—and to take care of sending out and paying bills and the rest of the paper work. He wouldn't even insist that his office help be young and pretty— God, he had all the sex he wanted or needed with Dolly. He'd settle for anybody who could type.

But it seemed as though even this modest dream was a long way from coming true. He did all right for himself, one way or another (some of them not too honest) but strictly as a lone wolf operator. True, he had connections with other detective outfits that let him farm out work at times when he had more than he could handle alone, but he'd never had even one operative working under him full time. He'd never get rich, but most of the time he thought it was best that way; when you work alone you can cut corners you wouldn't take the risk of telling someone else to cut for you. So in all probability the nearest he'd ever have to office help was what he had already, a telephone answering service. That was an absolute must, since he spent so little of his working time actually in the office; he couldn't have operated without it.

He took a deep drag of his cigarette, put it down on the edge of his desk, already scarred by a hundred cigarette bums, and went back to his typing. "Subject entered Crillon Bar at 3:15, looked around first, then went to the bar and ordered a drink. Talked, apparently casually, to the bartender while he drank it, but kept an eye on the door as though waiting for someone. At *3:25* the woman already described in previous report entered. She nodded to him and went to a booth. He joined her there and ordered drinks for both of them. At 3:47 he—"

The phone rang and he picked it up and said, "Mack Irby speaking."

"Mack." It was Dolly's voice. "Fletcher just left and—"

"All right," he said, interrupting her to save time. "I'll be around, but I'm going to finish this one report first. I'll be there in about—"

"Wait, Mack. It's not just that. He stole my jewelry, the few things I had in that leather box on my dresser. Not worth much, but— Do you think I should call the police and report it? And if I do, maybe you shouldn't come, maybe you shouldn't be here when they get here. What do you think I should do? Should I call the police?"

"Don't call the cops," he said flatly.

"But why not? Like I said, the stuff isn't worth much, but they might get it back for me."

"They might, Doll. But I might be able to do even better than that. Sit tight. This report can wait till tomorrow. I'll be there in five minutes. Just relax and don't worry."

He hung up the phone, got his hat and turned out the lights, locked the office, and left. Downstairs he got in his car. It was, as any car used for shadowing should be, inconspicuous—a five-year-old Studebaker Commander painted gray—but there was a bit of souping-up under the hood and it was kept in perfect condition; it could go over a hundred if it had to. He drove the dozen blocks to Dolly's in three minutes flat. He let himself into the building with the key he carried and it was exactly the five minutes he had predicted when he rapped lightly on Dolly's door. He heard her coming and called out, "It's me, Doll, Mack," to save her the business with the chain.

She let him in. She was still—or again—wearing the red kimono she'd put on when he'd left at nine, and he wondered if she'd have had sense enough to have dressed before she called police, if he had let her call them. He kissed her, and then firmly disentangled her.

"This is business," he said. "So no monkey-business. I'll sit here and you sit over there and don't distract me."

"All right, Mack honey. But can't I make us each a drink?"

"No, not— Well, all right. I can be asking questions while you make 'em." He sat down on the sofa and tossed his hat onto the end table. Dolly went behind the kitchenette's screen and he raised his voice a little so she could still hear him easily.

"So the family jewels are gone. Point one. Can you be absolutely positive this Fletcher took them? Obviously you missed them right after he left, but how long ago do you know for sure they were still in the box?"

"While you were still here, Mack, just before he came. Remember I had on those costume earrings—the ones with the green stones—and I took them off when I undressed. I hate earrings in bed, especially dangly ones. And I put them in the box on the dresser. The other things were there then too, or I'd have noticed."

"That makes it sure, all right. How come you missed the stuff so soon after he left? You weren't starting to get dressed again, were you?"

Dolly came around the screen, again with a glass in each hand and again the red kimono gaped open all the way down the front. Mack Irby took his drink from her and then resolutely averted his eyes. "Pull that damn kimono shut and sit down—over there. Now answer my last question."

Dolly sat down across from him and obediently pulled the top of the kimono closed. But she crossed her legs and it fell away from them; quite a lot of Dolly still showed. She said, "No, I wasn't going to get dressed again. I just—well, I just had a sudden hunch, right after he left and just before I called you, and I looked around to see if anything was gone. I looked in my purse first; there wasn't much money in it but it was still there, and then I looked in the jewelry box and it was empty and I knew my hunch had been right.

"You see, Mack, he was in an awful hurry and kind of— well, furtive is the word, I guess, when he left. Almost like he was scared. And besides that, he's in some kind of a jam over money. What he really came here for was to try to borrow some from me."

Mack Irby laughed shortly. "He sure didn't know you, Doll. What kind of money did he want? Did he mention an amount?"

"Five hundred. He offered to pay six back in a week or two. That would have been fair enough, if I knew him. But I probably don't even know his right name—and if Ray Fletcher *is* his right name he could still be planning to blow town for all I know."

"You played it smart, I'd say. Offering that much interest is suspicious, and besides, the, fact that he swiped your jewelry shows he ain't very honest. If you'd of lent him the money you'll never of got it back. Now you said the jewelry wasn't worth much. How much is not much?"

"Well, it was mostly costume stuff. Some of the things maybe cost up to twenty bucks apiece, but they wouldn't have any resale value. The wedding ring, worth ten or fifteen—I mean, that's what it would have cost new, not what he could get for it. And that diamond ring, the one with the flaw. You remember it."

Mack Irby remembered the ring. One of Dolly's "friends" had given it to her about a year ago. She'd turned it over to Mack to have appraised and maybe to sell it for her. It had *looked* like a good stone and as though it might weigh almost a carat; they'd thought it might be worth several hundred dollars. But the appraisal had been disappointing. Mack's jeweler friend had told him its diameter was deceptive; it was too shallow, cut too thin. And it had a bad flaw, one you could see with the naked eye if you looked at just the right angle. Seventy-five was all he offered for it. And at that price, since it looked to be worth much more, Dolly had decided to keep it.

Dolly seldom wore rings, but once in awhile someone wanted to take her out of town for a weekend, and if the someone was a free enough spender she sometimes went. Since they'd be Registering as man and wife she kept a plain wedding ring to wear on such occasions. And she thought that a diamond ring worn with it would look good and add verisimilitude.

Mack said, "If that's the lot, he won't get more than fifty bucks from a fence—if a fence would be willing to bother with the stuff at all. If he needs five hundred, he's in for a disappointment. All right, so much for the stuff. And now about Fletcher. I think we can take it for granted the name's a phony, or he wouldn't of risked robbing you."

He thought a moment.

"But there's still a possibility. If the jam he's in is so bad he's figuring on blowing town anyway, the name business might not worry him. Let's check something."

He walked over to the telephone table and picked up the directory and opened it. After a minute he said, "There's only one Ray Fletcher listed, a Ray W. Fletcher, seventy-one sixteen South Kramer. How long ago did your Ray Fletcher leave here?"

Dolly looked at her wrist watch—and was suddenly glad she'd kept it on instead of taking it off as she sometimes did. It was a good watch, worth more than all the items she'd lost put together. She said, "About fifteen minutes ago."

Mack said, "That address is to hell and gone on the south side. Take him at least half an hour to get there, so if that Ray Fletcher is home now we can eliminate him."

He picked up the phone and dialed. A man's voice answered, "Ray Fletcher speaking," and Mack said, "Sorry, wrong number," and put the phone down.

He went back to the sofa. "Not our boy; he's home. All right, what do we know about our boy? He told you he's a liquor salesman and I'd say that's probably true, account of his bringing you a case of whisky most of the times he brought you anything. Did he ever mention what outfit he works for?"

Dolly shook her head.

"The cartons the whisky came in. Were they stamped with the name of a distributor?"

"I didn't notice if they were. And the last carton got thrown out at least a month ago. But listen, the whisky was always Belle of Tennessee brand. Would that help? I mean, do all distributors handle all brands?"

"That might help. It'll pretty well pinpoint him if it's a brand his outfit has exclusive franchise for. But damn it, I won't be able to work that angle till tomorrow—and I want to get to him tonight if I possibly can, while he's still got the stuff on him. We won't be in such a strong position if he's got rid of it, or even stashed it somewhere."

He took another sip of his drink. "All right, Doll. Start at the beginning. Where and how did you meet the guy?"

"He called up one evening and said John Evans—that's a guy I was seeing once in a while then—had given him my name and phone number and suggested he give me a ring sometime. Wanted to know if he could drop up and meet me, and bring some liquor. I wasn't doing anything that evening and he sounded nice over the phone so I said sure."

"Know how to get in touch with this John Evans?"

"No. I don't know what happened but I haven't seen him in over a year."

"And John Evans was probably a phony name too. Damn it, Doll, this is a digression but you ought to know the right names of the men you see. Not for blackmail or anything—I know you don't go in for anything like that—but just for your own protection. Like tonight. You can do it. Sooner or later a guy gets in the can and leaves his pants outside and all you got to do is take a quick gander in his wallet for his right name and address. And from then on you'll know who he really is.

"But okay, let's get back to Ray Fletcher. Do you think he's married?"

"I'm almost sure. He never took me out anywhere, for one thing, just came to the apartment. Single guys—I know a few of them—like to show me around; I'm decorative. And another thing; he never stayed all night, usually left around twelve or one. And other little things—yeah, I'm sure he's married."

"Know what kind of a car he drives?"

She shook her head again. "He must drive one, but he never brought it upstairs with him."

"You sure don't know much about him. All right, physical description. Don't see how that'll help tonight, but we might as well get it over with."

"Well, he's about your build, maybe an inch taller."

"Go on."

She giggled. "He's about an inch taller, but you're about an inch longer, Mack."

He looked at her disgustedly. "A lot of help that is, unless I find him in a Turkish bath."

Suddenly he snapped his fingers. "Doll, was he wearing tonight a gray suit, white shirt, blue tie. Sandy hair, no hat?"

"How—? Oh, sure, you must have passed him on your way out. He got here just a minute after you left."

"Good. Then skip the rest of the description; I'll know him if I see him again. We passed in the doorway. But damn it, Doll, you haven't come up with anything yet that will let me find him tonight, and you gotta. Put down that drink and think hard. As many times as he was up here he must have said or done *something* that'd give me a lead. Think hard."

Dolly Mason closed her eyes and thought hard. After a minute she said, "He's a horse player. Usually had a racing form with him, in his pocket. At first, until I convinced him I don't bet, he used to give me tips on horses—and offered to place bets for me if I wanted to take the tips."

"Keep going."

Dolly's eyes opened wide. "Mack honey, I got something. I think Ray is his right *first* name."

"That helps. How do you know?"

"One evening, maybe six months ago, he must of made up his mind suddenly to make a bet. He used my phone to call some bookie to phone in the bet. Twenty bucks to win—I don't remember the horse or the track. He started out by saying 'This is Ray'; no last name but the bookie must have known him from that."

"Doll, we're getting somewhere. Think hard. Did he call the bookie by any name?"

"I think he did, but— Yeah, I remember. He said 'This is Ray, Joe,' and then went on and gave the bet."

Mack said, "I know two bookies named Joe. It couldn't be Joe Renfeld; he takes only cash bets, no phone business. Runs a cigar store and books on the side. So it's Joe Amico. I'll know in a minute."

He crossed to the telephone table, looked up a number and dialed it. When a voice answered he said, "This is Bill? Mack Irby. Is Joe there? Can I talk to him?"

Bill said sure and a minute later Joe's voice said, "Hi, Mack. What can I do you?"

"Joe, you got a customer named Ray. He's a liquor salesman. Can you give me the rest of his name?"

"What do you want with him, Mack? Listen, he owes me dough and if you're going to get him in trouble I'll never collect."

"It's the other way around," Mack said. "He's in trouble all right, but he'll be in worse trouble if I don't find him right away, tonight. He stole some jewelry from a client of mine. If I can get to him before he sells it, there'll be no beef; my client'll settle for getting the stuff back. If he fences it before I get to him, it'll be too late for that, see? I can find him tomorrow easy enough— how many liquor salesmen are there in town named Ray? But that might be too late to keep him out of jail."

Joe Amico grunted. "Guess you got a point. And I guess I pushed him too hard. All right, his last name's Fleck. F-l-e-c-k. I don't remember his address offhand, but it's in the phone book."

"Attaboy, Joe. You wouldn't make a guess which fence he might head for?"

"No, I wouldn't. I know some fences, and so do you, but I don't know which of 'em, if any, Ray might know or know about."

"Okay, one more thing. Got any idea where I might find him tonight? If the didn't head home, that is. I'll give his number a ring first."

"Best I could guess is some downtown tavern, almost any of them. He makes the rounds. Your best bet would be to make 'em too. Will you know him if you see him, Mack?"

"Yeah. Thanks to hell and back, Joe. So long."

He put down the phone and quickly looked up Ray Fleck in the phone book. He looked at the address first. Yes, it was close enough. If Fleck had headed straight for home he'd be there by now. And just maybe that's what he'd done, if he was scared.

He dialed the number and while it rang a dozen times he held his hand over the mouthpiece and spoke to Dolly. "Your boyfriend is Ray Fleck. Three-one-two Covington Place. But I guess he didn't head for home." He cradled the telephone. "So I go looking for him."

Dolly ran over to him, put her arms around his neck and pressed her body against his.

"Mack honey, do you have to start *right* away? Would fifteen or twenty minutes matter?"

Mack Irby laughed. "All right, I don't guess fifteen or twenty minutes will matter."

The red kimono fell almost completely away as he picked her up and carried her into the bedroom.

9:59 P.M.

Ray Fleck reached the edge of downtown afoot. He had walked in from Dolly's, not to save the price of a taxi—what would one lousy buck have mattered out of the thirteen that was all the cash he had left?—but simply because he hadn't seen a cruising cab. And by the time he reached the first place from which he could have phoned for one he was so near town that he knew he'd get there sooner if he kept on walking than if he phoned and waited for a cab.

He was still a bit scared at what he had done, but he was also excited. He didn't know what he had, and it might be anything. Maybe a thousand dollars' worth of stuff, for all he knew. At least a couple of hundred dollars' worth, he thought; the diamond ring alone, from the quick glimpse he got of it, ought to be worth at least that much, even at a fence's price. And he felt certain that it, at least, was genuine; people just don't put glass or a rhinestone into that kind of mounting, like an engagement ring. Or if they do, they use a chunk of glass or a rhinestone that's bigger and flashier, one that looks like a three-carat diamond instead of a one-carat one. But the other stuff could be anything. Oh, probably some of it was costume jewelry, but if even a few pieces were real, he'd settle happily. And if the green stones in those earrings were emeralds they'd be worth at least twice what the diamond was worth. Maybe more. Each of the two stones was at least twice the size of the diamond, and he thought he remembered having heard that good emeralds cost just about as much per carat as diamonds.

Several times he'd been tempted, after he was out of the immediate neighborhood of the scene of his crime and over the worst of his initial panic, to stop under a street light and take a look at what he had, but he resisted the impulse. He didn't know a thing about jewelry and not even a close examination under a bright light would really tell him anything. If some of the pieces were marked *14K* and others *gold filled* it would give him a clue but it would tell him nothing about the stones and the stones were what counted.

He might as well hunt Fats Davis right away and let Fats make the appraisal. He'd thought of Fats even before he'd lifted Dolly's jewelry, while he was still making up his mind whether to or not.

He was reasonably sure Fats was a fence. Several people had told him so and he had no reason not to believe them. He didn't know Fats very well but he thought Fats knew him well enough to trust him and do business with him if he did buy and sell hot ice. At any rate, Fats would be able to make an appraisal for him; Fats, whatever his business was now, had been a jeweler once. Everybody knew that much about him.

He might have trouble finding Fats because he didn't know his right first name. He wouldn't be listed in the phone book under *Davis, Fats,* and there'd probably be a hundred or more Davises in the book, too many to try phoning down the line.

But Fats hung out around the downtown joints and there was an even chance he'd run into him if he made the rounds. And if he didn't find Fat he'd be sure sooner or later to run into someone who knew him well enough to tell him how to make contact, or who at least would know Fats's first name.

Jick Walters' place would be the best bet; he'd run into Fats oftener there than in any other tavern. And Jick at least knew Fats, although Ray didn't know how well.

He headed for Jick's, but since there were two other taverns he had to pass on the way, he made a quick stop in each of them. Business was slow in both; there were only a few customers and none of them people he knew. But he knew both bartenders and asked them about Fats. Neither of them knew a thing and so he pushed on down the street.

Business was slow at Jick's, too, but at least Jick himself was behind the bar pulling tap. He waited till he'd ordered a drink and Jick had made it for him before he broached the subject.

"Jick, I'm looking for Fats Davis. But I don't know his first name so I can't find him in the phone book. You know how I can get in touch with him? It's important."

"Yeah, I know," Jick said.

"How?"

Jick grinned. "Turn right and walk a dozen steps. He's in the end booth down there."

Ray looked that way. He'd thought the booth was empty, but he realized now that Fats's head wouldn't show over the top of the partition. Fats was almost literally a five-by-five. He wasn't more than two inches over five feet and couldn't have been more than a few inches under five feet around the waist.

"Swell," Ray said. "What's he drinking? I'll take one over to him."

"Straight shots. But go ahead, Ray. I'll bring his drink over."

"Thanks, Jick." Ray picked up his own drink and strolled back. "Hi, Fats," he said. "Can I talk to you a minute?"

Fats's little eyes weren't especially cordial when he looked up, but he nodded, and Ray slid into the other side of the booth, facing the front of the tavern.

"Want to ask you how much some stuff is worth," Ray said. "And if by any chance you want, to buy it, that'll be swell."

"Got it with you?"

Ray nodded. "But I ordered you a drink when Jick told me you were here. Let's wait till he's—"

But Jick was already there with a shot and a chaser and, put them down on the table. When Ray had paid him and he'd gone back behind the bar, Fats asked, "More than one piece?"

"Yeah," Ray said, and reached for his pocket.

But Fats said, "Wait a minute," and took a clean handkerchief from his pocket, unfolded it and spread it in front of him. "Put it on this," he said, "so one of us can pick it up in one grab if somebody starts back this way. You're facing front; slide over to the outer edge of your seat so you can watch that way."

Ray took the crumpled handkerchief out of his pocket first and then managed to get hold of all the jewelry at once. He put it in the middle of Fats's spread handkerchief and then, as Fats had suggested, slid over to where he could watch toward the front of the tavern. He didn't think anybody would head back—there were only four other customers in the place—but it was best to play safe.

But he watched Fats out of a corner of his eye. Fats stirred through the stuff with a stubby index finger. He picked up one of the earrings with the green stones first, looked at it closely and then put it down again. He felt glad things had worked out this way, that Fats hadn't made him tell what he thought he had to sell. If the earrings were glass it would have made things embarrassing if he'd told Fats they were emeralds. And the other way around would have been worse. If he'd told Fats it was all costume jewelry except the diamond, then Fats could cheat him all too easily if the stones really were emeralds.

Fats picked up the diamond ring and took a jeweler's loupe from his pocket. He screwed the loupe into his right eye and studied the diamond through it. Briefly. Then he put the ring back with the other pieces and the loupe back in his pocket. He wadded up the handkerchief and pushed it across to Ray Fleck.

"Put it in your pocket," he said. "It's all junk. What did you think *I* could do with it? Keep the handkerchief. Fair trade for the drink."

He picked up his shot and tossed it down, took a short sip from the water chaser and then wiped the thick lips with the back of his hand.

"My God, Fats," Ray said. "You trying to tell me that isn't even a diamond in that ring? I know the other stuff is costume jewelry, but—" He did know it now.

"Sure, it's a diamond. *What* a diamond. Got a flaw in it you could crawl inside, and it's a cheater cut, thin like a poker chip."

"You mean it's not worth *anything?*"

Fats Davis shrugged. "Maybe fifty bucks, mounting and all. It's not too bad a mounting."

Ray Fleck was stunned, but he didn't doubt that Fats was telling the truth. Of course Dolly, smart little bitch that she was, wouldn't keep anything valuable right on top of her dresser where any man who visited her could swipe it—as easily as he had. If she owned anything valuable in the way of jewelry she'd at least keep it out of sight and probably locked up at that.

Well, anyway, fifty bucks would again put him in shape to sit in on the poker. He sighed. "Okay, Fats. I'll settle for fifty bucks."

Fats shook his head. "Huh-uh. I don't want it. I said the ring might be worth that—but I don't mess with peanut stuff. You take as much risk and don't make anything."

"What risk?" Ray asked. "Damn it, Fats, I didn't steal this stuff. It's mine." He realized that sounded silly. "My wife's, I mean, but this is a community property state and that makes it mine too."

"I'll buy that," Fats said. "But does she know you're selling it? There could still be a beef. She misses it and calls copper, and you got to go along with her, or confess up. And tell what you did with the stuff—and that gets my name on the blotter even if they can't hang a rap on me. Huh-uh, Fleck." He shook his head again. "If the stuff was worth a couple of grand, I'd take a chance maybe, but not for junk jewelry."

"Fats, she knows about it, gave it to me to see if I could get anything out of it when I told her I was in a jam. Listen, the costume pieces are stuff she was tired of. And she was married before, and the engagement and wedding rings are from her first marriage—and that's how come neither of us knew the diamond wasn't as good as it looked. We never had it appraised or anything."

"Take it to a hock shop if it's a clean deal. They'll give you as much as I offered on the diamond, and maybe even a little something on the other junk. Like the wedding band; you'll get old gold value for that, if nothing more."

"But damn it, Fats. I need the money tonight. The hock shops are closed."

Fats sighed. "All right, get your wife on the phone and let me talk to her. If she says she gave you that ring to sell I'll buy it. Otherwise no dice."

"She's out with friends, damn it. I can't reach her on the phone. But I'm telling you the truth, Fats."

Fats slid out of the booth and stood up. "Sorry, pal. No dice." He turned to the front and said, "Oh-oh. Fuzz. Better get that back in your pocket. I'm getting out of here."

Looking past Fats as he walked to the front, Ray saw that two uniformed policemen had just come in. One of them he knew, Hoff. The other he knew by sight as Hoff's partner. A momentary chill went down his spine, but then he realized they couldn't possibly be looking for him. Not possibly. Just the same, he was relieved when Hoff caught his eye and waved a hand casually, then stopped at the bar with his partner.

He quickly stuffed the handkerchief with the junk jewelry back in his pocket and stood up. He wanted to get out of here too, although he didn't know yet where he was going.

He intended to walk past the two policemen but Hoff stopped him by turning as he approached and saying, "Hi, Ray. Have a drink." And it would have looked funny if he'd turned it down.

"Thanks, sure," he said. "How goes it?"

Hoff nodded to Jick and then turned back. "Hell of a night. The psycho's out. Every squad car we've got is out and they're ordering us round like crazy. We dropped in for a quickie."

He had to pretend to be interested. "You mean he's killed another dame."

"No, not yet, but he's on the prowl. Made a try late this afternoon. Dame alone in a flat on Koenig. Knocked on the door and called out 'Western Union,' and she opened up— but on a chain. When he saw or heard the chain he ran fast; she didn't get a look at him. She phoned in, but he was out of the neighborhood by the time we got there."

"Sounds like it was him all right," Ray said. Jick had-put a drink in front of him and he said, "Thanks," and lifted his glass to Hoff.

Hoff said, "And he made another try just a little while ago—or we think it was him, anyway. Must of decided women weren't opening doors for him any more. Dame in a cottage out on

Autremont heard someone trying to break in a window and phoned in. Nobody when we got there—but there were chisel marks on a window, so she wasn't imagining things."

"That could have been a burglar, couldn't it?"

"Burglars don't break in lighted places with someone inside. He could of seen her from the window he tried. And the phone too. Quit trying the window and ran when he saw her dialing."

Hoff's partner leaned around him. "Well, we know now he drives a car, anyway. She heard it start up while she was still talking over the phone." He clunked down his glass. "Hoffy, we gotta go. This was a quickie, remember?"

"Can't I buy you boys one?" Ray Fleck asked.

Hoff said, "Thanks, Ray, but no. We're taking a chance being outa the squad car this long. If the radio operator calls our number and we don't answer, we're on the carpet for dereliction of duty. So long."

They went out. Ray looked at his glass and was surprised to find that it was empty. Morosely, for lack of a better idea, for lack of any place to go or anything else to do, he put money on the bar and said, "One more, Jick."

Jick picked up the glass. "Anything wrong, Ray? You look kind of—well, not so good."

"Everything's wonderful," Ray said. "It's a great, wide wonderful world."

Except, where was he going to get four hundred and eighty bucks by tomorrow night?

10:25 P.M.

Benny Knox had left his newsstand early; usually he didn't leave until eleven o'clock or when he'd sold out on papers, whichever came first. But tonight at a quarter after ten there'd been only a few papers left and he'd decided not to wait any longer; he'd waited that long only because Mr. Hoff had told him to finish out the evening and then go to the police station to turn himself in. That had disappointed him; he had hoped that Mr. Hoff and his partner would take him in themselves in the squad car, with the siren going and the red light flashing. He had had rides in automobiles only a few times in his life and never one in a squad car.

Now inside the police station he stood in front of the tall receiving desk, at which a gray-haired man was busily writing. The man hadn't looked up yet. That is, he'd looked up when Benny had come in but then had looked down and started writing again. Benny stood there waiting and feeling awkward, but he didn't want to interrupt the man. Under Benny's arm was clutched the cigar box, now with a rubber band around it, that held his receipts for the day. One thing about the money in it puzzled him. He'd counted it before he left the stand, because he always did, and there were about ten dollars less in it than there should have been. He couldn't figure out what could have happened to ten dollars—except for a vague recollection of someone laughing at him; he remembered feeling angry about that but he couldn't remember who the someone had been or how it connected with the ten dollars.

The gray-haired man at the desk put down his pen but he still didn't look toward Benny. He picked up the telephone and said into it, "Get me Burton." And then a few seconds later, "Lieu-

tenant, Benny Knox is here. Shall I send him on upstairs, or—"
And then, "Okay."

He put down the phone and looked at Benny. "The lieutenant
wants to talk to you, in his office." He jerked a thumb. "Down
that corridor, second door on your right."

Benny found the door and knocked on it lightly. He opened it
and went in when a voice called out for him to do so. The
lieutenant with the red hair was back of a desk.

He said, "Sit down, Benny. Officer Hoff radioed in earlier that
you want to confess to two murders. Is that right?"

Benny sat down. "Yes, sir, Lieutenant. I did kill them women,
both of them. I choked 'em to death." He held up the evidence—
his hands.

The red-haired lieutenant nodded gravely. "Benny, we'll have to
hold you overnight and Doc Kranz will talk to you tomorrow. What
happens after that depends on what he says. Do you understand?"

Benny nodded. Although he didn't see where a doctor came
in, that didn't matter as long as they were going to put him in jail
and punish him. Then God and his father would forgive him and
everything would be all right.

The lieutenant said, "One thing, Benny. That woman who
takes care—that you stay with. Does she know you were coming
here? If not, I'll phone her to save her worrying when you don't
come home tonight."

Benny shook his head, feeling ashamed of not having thought
about Mrs. Saddler. She *would* worry about him. And wait up.
She never went to bed until he got home.

"Let's see," the lieutenant said, reaching to pull the phone
book over in front of him. "Her name's Saddler, isn't it? And on
Fergus Street?"

"I got her number here, sir," Benny said, glad of a chance to be
helpful. He took a card from his pocket and handed it across the
desk. It was an "in case of accident or illness, notify" card with
Mrs. Saddler's name, address, and phone number on it. She'd
asked him to carry it always and once in a while asked him to
show it to her so she'd be sure he hadn't lost it.

"Thanks, Benny." The lieutenant took the card and gave the number on it to the switchboard operator over the phone. And then he was saying, "Hello, Mrs. Saddler? I'm phoning you about Benny—this is Lieutenant Burton speaking—so you won't worry when he doesn't get home tonight.

"Yes, he's here and he's just confessed to the two murders—the two recent sex killings—and… Yes, I know he didn't do them. We're not charging him with them. But you remember what I explained to you about a year ago—that if Benny ever confessed to anything again we'd have to hold him until Dr. Kranz has a chance to talk to… No, I wouldn't dare call the doctor tonight; the chief would have my ears if I did… Sometime tomorrow, and we'll try to get him to make it early enough so Benny won't lose the whole day if Doc says to… Oh, no, Mrs. Saddler, it wouldn't do any good at all for you to come down. We wouldn't be able to let you see him anyway, tonight. But we'll take good care of him, and we'll phone you again tomorrow as soon as there's anything to report. I won't be on duty then, but I'll leave a memo… All right, I'll tell him. Goodnight, Mrs. Saddler."

He put the phone down and smiled at Benny. "She said to tell you good night for her, and for *you* not to worry. You've got a fine friend there, Benny."

Benny nodded. He did feel sorry about Mrs. Saddler and that she'd never see him again unless she visited him in jail. She was like a mother to him, or the nearest to a mother he'd ever known. Then he remembered something the lieutenant said to her.

"But, Lieutenant, sir, you told her I didn't do it. I *did*, honestly, I remember, I choked them. You got to believe me."

"Just a minute, Benny," the lieutenant said. He picked up the phone again. "Give me the jail—Wait, don't. Just call them yourself and tell them to send down a couple of boys to pick up a customer, in my office. Thanks."

He looked back at Benny. "Now Benny listen. Maybe you're not yet in the mood to believe *me*, but I'm going to tell you this anyway. I like you and I hope you get by Doc Kranz again, and I think you'll have a better chance of doing that if I can get you started thinking straight tonight. Then maybe tomorrow you'll realize how wrong you were thinking.

"Listen, Benny, we *know* you didn't commit those murders, and I'll tell you how we know. After each one of them we checked a hell of a lot of suspects. Every man who had a record of sex offenses, any kind. Every known psychopath, everyone known to us to be seriously abnormal or subnormal mentally. You—uh—"

"I know I'm not very bright, Lieutenant. I don't mind your saying so as long as you don't laugh at me. I don't like people to laugh at me."

"I'm not laughing, Benny. Listen to me, listen hard. We checked you on both of them. On one you've got an absolutely solid alibi; you *couldn't* have done it. We know just when that one happened, ten o'clock in the evening. We could rule you out without even leaving the station, because Hoff remembered it was ten o'clock, within a few minutes, when he picked up a paper from you at your stand, three miles or so from where the woman was being killed. Your alibi on the other murder isn't quite so solid, because we don't know exactly what time it happened. But we know you were at your stand all evening till eleven and you got home about twenty after, just the time it takes you to walk that far. We can't prove you didn't sneak out later, of course— but you *didn't*, Benny. Whoever killed either one of those women killed both of them. That's for sure if anything is."

Benny looked and felt miserable. The lieutenant didn't believe him, and neither had Mr. Hoff. That much at least of the lieutenant's speech had registered.

He said unhappily. "But I *did* kill them, both of them. I remember, Lieutenant. I'm sure."

"You just think you're sure, Benny. Now before you go to sleep tonight and in the morning after you wake up you think over what I said and make yourself a little less sure. I—"

The door opened and two men in the uniforms of turnkeys from the city jail on the upper floors of the building came in. One of them, the tall one, said, "Package for us, Lieutenant? You through with him?"

The lieutenant sighed. "Yeah, I guess I'm through with him. This is Benny Knox, boys. He'll be your guest tonight. A disposition order will come up sometime tomorrow."

"Sure. Just in the tank?"

"Hell, no. Benny never took a drink in his life; don't put him in with the drunks. You've got cell space, haven't you?"

"Yeah. What's with the cigar box he's got? A time bomb set to go off at midnight?"

"It's got money in it," the lieutenant said. "And be sure there's the same amount when you turn it in."

The tall turnkey grinned. "Why, Lieutenant! Have you frisked him otherwise?"

"No, Benny wouldn't be carrying a—Oh, I suppose we might as well protect ourselves by following the routine. He just might get a funny idea, at that. You take care of it."

"All right, chum," the turnkey said to Benny. "Come on; we'll take care of you. We'll give you the bridal suite, and you can be making up your mind whether you want a blonde or a brunette to go with it."

Benny realized that was a joke so he didn't try to answer. He went with them along two corridors and up several flights in an elevator, then along another corridor and through a door into an office in which there was a desk with a young male clerk behind it.

At the desk they asked him for the cigar box; they opened it and the clerk counted it. When he called out and wrote down the total, it was the same amount Benny himself had counted it to be just before he'd left the newsstand. Meanwhile the turnkeys had asked him to empty his pockets onto the desk and he had. They patted him a few places and then gave him back what he'd taken out of his pockets except for one thing, a small penknife he used for cutting the rope around bundles of papers and for cleaning his fingernails. They asked him to take off his belt and he did. He wasn't wearing a necktie; he never wore one except to church. And they didn't take his shoelaces because he was wearing moccasins. Hard shoes hurt his feet and he always wore moccasins except on Sunday.

Then they took him down another corridor, through a steel door, past the barred doors of cells. Then they opened a cell door and the tall turnkey said, "All right, chum, this is it. Home, sweet home."

Benny went in and they closed the door behind him. The closing door made a loud clang and someone somewhere yelled out, "Quiet, you bastards!" And then they went away and left him alone.

The cell was long and narrow, about six feet by fifteen. Enough light came in from the corridor through the bars so he could see his way around. There was a double-decker bunk bed—with no one in either the upper nor the lower—two chairs and, back in the far corner, a commode. That was all, or it was all that he could see now, in the dimness.

He sighed and took off his suit coat, hung it over the back of one of the chairs and put his moccasins under the chair.

He started to get into the lower bunk and then remembered that he'd never slept in a high bed, an upper bunk, in his life and he wondered if it would feel any different, so he climbed into the upper and stretched himself out.

The lieutenant had told him there was something he should think about tonight and he tried to remember what it was. But within seconds, and before he could remember, he was asleep.

Ray Fleck still stood at the bar in Jick's, where Hoff and his partner had left him, nursing a drink and moodily making wet circles on the bar with the bottom of his glass. Twice Jick, who wasn't very busy, had said something to him but he'd answered briefly and without looking up so Jick knew he hadn't wanted to talk and had moved along the bar to someone else. Years of tending bar taught him when to leave a guy alone to brood over his drink.

He was thinking about the poker game that would be starting soon now and he was blowing hot and cold on the idea of trying to get into it. There was still one chance that he could: the diamond ring. It was a strictly cash game, no checks cashed and no borrowing. But he might be able to make an exception to the borrowing rule if he had security like that to offer. Sure, he could. He remembered now one night when Luke Evarts had gone broke and had managed to keep going a while by borrowing thirty-five bucks from Doc Corwin, putting up as security an almost new and quite expensive wrist watch. And the diamond ring, damn it, *looked* good, looked like it ought to be worth several hundred dollars, and none of the boys was a jeweler or carried a magnifying glass. One of them might be willing to lend him a hundred on it, or at least fifty.

Of course it would be embarrassing as hell to have to go up there to Harry Brambaugh's flat with no money at all and have to try to raise money, on whatever security, to get into the game. Much more embarrassing than going there with a reasonable amount of money and raising more, as Luke had done with the wrist watch, after losing it. It would really be embarrassing if he went there and was unable to play at all, if no one would lend him even fifty on the damn ring.

But that wasn't the important reason why he was beginning to blow cold on the poker. In as bad a jam as he was in a little embarrassment, losing a little face, was something he could put up with. If he didn't raise Amico's money he was going to lose worse than face. He was beginning to worry about his luck, as far as tonight was concerned. Everything, but everything, had gone sour on him (he thought; he didn't know that his real troubles hadn't started yet). Bad luck runs in streaks and he didn't have the slightest indication that his was going to change tonight.

And a better idea had come to him, standing there at the bar.

He could go home soon, even now, and be there, sober, when Ruth got home around midnight. She'd be surprised to see him, after their quarrel, and maybe even pleased, if she was over her mad.

But whether she was still mad or not he wouldn't let it develop into a quarrel again. He'd be calm and patient with her, and he'd be able to explain this time what he'd not been able to explain this afternoon—exactly what Joe Amico's ultimatum had been, exactly what Joe's deadline was and what he'd do if the money wasn't given him by then. She'd listen; he'd *make* her listen. She was a stubborn bitch all right and that damned policy was the thing she was most stubborn about, but she *did* have common sense. If he could explain to her and convince her, and he thought he could, that his keeping his job depended completely on his having five hundred dollars tomorrow, she'd at least see that her own selfish interests were in this case identical with his.

Jick Walters was across the bar from him again. He didn't say anything but he glanced interrogatively at Ray's glass, and Ray saw it was empty. Ray nodded, and put money on the bar while Jick made him another drink.

He could do it, he thought. He could talk Ruth into it—if he could avoid losing his temper and stay calm and reasonable, keep her that way. And thank God the home office of her insurance company was right here; they could go to it together any time tomorrow and she'd be able to get a check while they waited. No sweat at all about Amico's deadline; he wouldn't wait till evening to get the money to him.

It would work. He wondered why he hadn't thought of it sooner, right after Amico had read the riot act to him, instead of wasting time trying first to borrow money from Dolly, and then stealing her junky jewelry. He'd get rid of that tomorrow, too, if Ruth was reasonable about the insurance business. He'd mail it back to Dolly—and then call her up and tell her he'd done so, apologize, and explain. And if she was reasonable about it and not too mad, he'd even be able to see her again sometime, when he was solvent again.

But handling Ruth came first. He found himself planning what he'd say to her as he'd plan a sales talk. He'd have to eat a little crow, and make some promises. Not to quit gambling; she'd never believe him if he promised that, and disbelief would antagonize her. But he would promise—and sincerely, because he never wanted to get into a jam like this again—never again to gamble on credit and go in over his head. He could promise too to pay back the loan against the policy at, say, twenty-five a week, so the full ten thousand would be coming when the endowment was due. And even make the payments for a few weeks until things were on even keel again. He could tell her—

"Beg your pardon, Mr. Fleck. Like to talk to you."

He'd been aware, while thinking, of someone coming up alongside him at the bar and ordering and getting a drink, and now he turned to see who it was. He didn't know the guy. Medium height, stocky and husky-looking, reddish face, and eyes like pale blue marbles.

"You don't know me," the man said. "My name's Mack Irby."

Ray Fleck nodded, not too cordially.

"Glad to know you, Mr. Kirby," he said. "Got to leave in a minute but—what's it about?"

"Irby, not Kirby. Mack Irby—does sound like Kirby when you say both names together. Look, it's kind of private. End booth back there's empty, and so's the one next it. Let's go back to the end booth."

Mack raised his arm and motioned to the back of the room. The movement drew Ray's gaze to the dark corner near the commode.

Ray frowned. "I said I got just a minute. You can tell me what it's about right here." The guy might be a damn insurance salesman, for all he knew. Or more likely a bill collector.

Irby said, "Let's say I want to talk about a friend of yours, Mr. Fleck. His name's something like yours. It's Ray Fletcher."

Ray Fleck winced. He knew that the wince was visible, even obvious, but he couldn't help it; the shock had been too great. Here was trouble, new trouble, just when he'd thought he had figured a safe answer to the problem of his debt to the bookie. Now this. He had no doubt what it concerned. At various times in his life and for various reasons he'd used. a name other than his own, but not always the same one; to no one but Dolly Mason had he ever given his name as Fletcher.

But how had he been found so quickly? The only thing he could think of was that Dolly must have known all along, or for a long time, what his real identity was. There'd been times—not tonight—when she'd been briefly alone with his clothes while he'd gone into the bathroom; on any of those occasions she could have taken a quick look at identification in his wallet or papers in his pocket. Just what a girl like Dolly would do. Why hadn't he thought of...

"Well, Fleck?" There was an edge of impatience in Irby's voice now. "Want to talk in the back booth, or down at headquarters?"

"The booth," Ray said. His voice didn't come out quite right. But he picked up his glass and started toward the rear of the tavern. And a sudden thought came and with it a sudden hope that this wasn't as bad a jam as he bad feared. It wasn't a pinch— at least not yet. The cop—he *must* be a cop; he looked and acted like one—hadn't simply pinched him; he wanted to talk, and in private.

That meant Dolly hadn't simply called the police, given his name and description and reported the theft. She hadn't wanted the publicity, for obvious reasons. This Irby must be a friend of hers on the force—either a plain-clothes cop or a regular cop who was off duty when she called him. And she'd have told him she didn't want to make a complaint if she could get her stuff back without making one. Thank God, he thought, Fats Davis hadn't bought any of the stuff after all, and he still had it intact, ready to hand back. If he'd sold the ring for fifty they'd claim it was worth more and there'd still be trouble.

But, he thought as he slid into the booth, he'd let Irby talk first. He wouldn't make the mistake he'd made with Amico earlier by talking out of turn, admitting to having dragged down Connolly's thirty-buck bet when Sam-the-waiter's smaller bet was the only one Amico had known about. Just conceivably, although he didn't see how, this current deal didn't even concern the jewelry at all.

Irby slid in across from him, where Fats had sat only half an hour ago.

Irby said, "Keep your hands on top of the table, Fleck. The stuff's in your left pants pocket—you unconsciously put your hand over it while you were walking back to make sure it was still there. And I wouldn't want you to try to get any idea of ditching it here in the booth. I'd have to take you in right away if you tried that."

It was the jewelry then, all right. And there wasn't any use in his denying it—or of volunteering any information either. Ray Fleck just nodded. And kept his hands in sight.

Irby said, "All right, I'll put my cards on the table. Or my card." He took a card from the breast pocket of his coat and put it down in front of Ray. *Mack Irby, Private investigator.* And an address and a phone number. "Put it in your pocket. You might want to use me sometime to get you out of a jam. But not *this* jam; I've already got a client. And you can guess who it is, without straining yourself."

Ray Fleck nodded again. And to avoid discussion and keep things moving he put the card into his own breast pocket.

"Meanwhile," Irby said, "don't let the fact that I'm a private detective and not a cop dazzle you into thinking I can't arrest you, or that I won't if I have to. I carry a deputy's badge, for one thing. And if I didn't I can still make a citizen's arrest if I find someone in the act of committing a crime. And you are; you're in possession of stolen property. And if you think I can't handle you—" He pulled back his coat far enough so Ray could see the butt of a flat automatic in a shoulder holster. "Just don't try to make a run for it."

"I'm not running," Ray said. "But you wouldn't shoot a man for—"

"In the leg I would. Try me and see."

"Look, Irby," Ray said. "You don't want to arrest me or you would have right away. Dolly just wants her junk back, and I'm willing to give it back. I've still got it all. So why don't I just give it to you and call it square. And you can give her my apologies too."

"It's not that simple, Fleck. My client will settle for restitution—but full restitution, and the way she wants it. You know how women are. They get tired of clothes and of jewelry and would rather have new things than old ones. She'd much rather have the cash value of that jewelry than the stuff itself back, so she could buy new to replace it. And there's the matter of the fee I'll have to charge her. I think she should be reimbursed for that, don't you?"

Ray Fleck licked his suddenly dry lips. "Is this a shakedown, blackmail? If it is, it won't work. I'm broke, flat broke and in debt already."

"Let's take, those points one at a time, Fleck. First, blackmail. Blackmail is a crime. If you think I'm trying to blackmail you, you can arrest me. Citizen's arrest. And I'll arrest you for grand larceny and we'll handcuff ourselves together—I've got cuffs, right in my hip pocket—and go in to headquarters and accuse each other. I can make my charge stick, especially if I don't let you get rid of what's in your pocket, and I assure you I won't let you. Your charge would be your word against mine, and my word's damned good down there. They'd laugh at you. Shall we do it that way?"

Ray Fleck put out a hand for his glass but the hand trembled and he put it down on the table again. "All right, you've got me. But damn it, you can't get blood out of a turnip. I *am* broke. I—"

Irby put up a hand to stop him.

"I know quite a bit more about you, Fleck, than I did when I started looking for you a little less than an hour ago. You weren't in the first five bars I tried, but the bartender or owner knew you in every one of them. I know you're married. And I know which outfit you sell for—J. and B. and that you've been with them for quite a while. Nobody guessed your income at less than a hundred a week and most thought more. So, broke at the moment or not, I figure you can raise the money somehow—and I don't care how you do it—to make adequate restitution to Miss Mason. And I figure the amount should be a nice even thousand dollars."

At the expression on Ray's face, Irby raised a hand. "I don't know whether you've tried to fence the stuff as yet. If you have, you're aware it won't bring anything like that sum. But don't forget there's a terrific difference between a fence's price, and a retail jeweler's. And Miss Mason will be replacing those items at retail; I'd say it will cost her five hundred dollars, or almost that. Say that half of the other five hundred is my fee—and I'm sure you'll agree that under the circumstances that shouldn't come out of Miss Mason's pocket. Call the other half punitive damages, or payment for the mental anguish Miss Mason suffered in learning that a friend whom she'd trusted turned out to be a sneak thief. Break it down any way you like, but that's the amount it's going to add up to."

Ray Fleck said bitterly, "it *is* blackmail then. Damn you, Irby, I'm tempted—"

"To spend six months in jail—and lose your job, your friends, and probably your wife if she's worth anything to you? Just to save a lousy grand?"

Irby leaned forward to reach into his left hip pocket and brought out a pair of handcuffs. "I tried to give you a break," he said, "but if you'd rather go to jail, let's get it over with."

Ray said miserably,' "You win. But—how long will I have to raise it? It may take me—"

"We'll worry about that later. For tonight, if you want to walk out of here free, two painless steps are all you got to do. First, write a check for a thousand dollars made out to Miss Dolly Mason, date it today." He held up a hand to stop Ray's protest. "Don't tell me you haven't got a thousand in your account. I'll concede that, or you wouldn't be broke. I'll tell my client when to cash it. Let me worry about that."

Ray said sullenly, "I've got a dollar and some cents in the account, just enough to hold it open. All right. But I've got to get my wallet out of my hip pocket to get a check." Irby nodded, and he took out his wallet and took from it one of several blank checks he kept folded in one of the compartments. Irby offered him a pen, but he shook his head and took his own from his inside coat pocket, and wrote the check.

"Don't put the pen away," Irby told him. "One more step." He read the check carefully and put it into his own wallet. Then he took from his coat pocket a folded sheet of blank paper. He unfolded it and put it in front of Ray Fleck. "Now a confession. Put the date down and I'll dictate the rest."

"Confession! My God, you've got the check. Why do you want a confession too?"

"Think, Fleck. We might have to prove what that check' was given for. Maybe you haven't thought of this yet, but you will: If I let you walk out of here free what's to prevent you from ditching the stolen property down the nearest sewer right away— and then, first thing tomorrow morning, stopping payment on the check? And if she tried to make trouble your story—you'd think of it—would be you'd given her the check on a drunken generous impulse and had reconsidered, especially when you sobered up and realized you didn't have money in the bank to cover it. Be embarrassing for you to have to tell a story like that, but how could Dolly disprove it?"

Ray Fleck understood and nodded miserably; his mind *had* been playing around with some such idea, although he hadn't worked out the details yet. He wrote down the date. And what Irby dictated to him after that. It wasn't long, but, it sewed him up completely and left no loopholes. It even accounted for the fact that restitution was being made by check instead of return of the jewelry by stating that he had already disposed of several items of the stolen property. It didn't incriminate Dolly in any way by implying that he had ever been intimate with her.

He signed it and pushed it across. Irby folded the paper and put it in his pocket. He said, "Okay, you can have this back when my client has cashed the check."

Ray Fleck stared miserably down into his glass, not wanting to look at his tormentor. It was going to take him months, he was thinking, to get himself out of this, even if Ruth came through and took him off the hook on his gambling debt.

He heard Irby slide out of the booth. And then, standing outside, Irby bent over the end of the booth table. "By the way, Fleck," he said, "you owe Joe Amico some money too. That's only a gambling debt and this is a larceny rap. This comes first. Understand?"

Startled, Ray looked up, into those light blue marble- like eyes. He said, "Good God, man, I've got only till tomorrow evening on that. I can't possibly raise a thousand in a day. It'll take me weeks."

"It better not," Irby said. "This comes ahead of a gambling debt, and I'm not kidding. If you're paying off Amico tomorrow evening, you're paying this off sooner. Tomorrow's Friday, and it's not going to wait over the weekend. Your bank closes at three tomorrow, and Miss Mason will be there just before then with the check. If it's 'insufficient funds' the confession and the check both go to the police."

"God, Irby. I can't possibly—"

"You better, and I don't care how. See a loan shark, sell your house, your car or your wife, anything. Rob a bank for all I care. But this check will be presented for cashing at your bank at three tomorrow."

He turned and walked away, as casually as though he hadn't left a desperate man behind him. Ray Fleck reached for his drink. His hand shook badly but there was so little left in the glass that he didn't spill any. He drank it at a gulp.

He wanted to get out, away from everybody, to walk the night alone and try to think, *to think*. But he wanted Irby to have time to get clear first. He strode to, the front of the tavern and stood looking out of the window. He saw Irby get into a car parked across the street and drive away.

Then he himself left, and walked. Not even a car to drive in tonight, he thought, feeling sorry for himself, and as though thinking about that one little trouble would help him forget his *real* troubles. But he didn't dare try to forget them, he realized; he had to find an answer. If there was an answer.

He saw an open sewer grating at the first corner and for a moment he was tempted to push the damned jewelry, handkerchief and all, through it. But the thought came to him that that would be a useless gesture now. With the written confession in Irby's hands, soon in Dolly's, having the stuff on him was no additional danger to him now. Besides, it was worth *something*. If a fence had considered giving him fifty for the ring, probably a hock shop proprietor would give him at least that and maybe more tomorrow. And since the police didn't have a list for checking there'd be no danger selling the ring openly now. No use throwing fifty bucks or more down the sewer. Maybe *Uncle* would give him a few bucks, say five for all of it, for the costume stuff.

He thought again of the ring in connection with the poker game. The game would be starting by now. But—oh, hell, it was hopeless. He needed fifteen hundred now, fourteen hundred and eighty to be exact, and he'd never seen money like that change hands in the game. A few hundred, never more than five or six, was as much as he'd ever seen anybody win or lose, and not that much very often. It would have been a miracle if he'd have got in the game and won enough to pay off Amico.

His only chance, his *only* chance, now was Ruth and her insurance policy. (What if she'd get killed by a car on the way home from work tonight? He'd have the whole ten thousand coming, as her beneficiary, and his troubles would be gone. Eight and a half thousand left after paying off one and a half thousand. But things like that never happened, not when you desperately needed to have them happen.) But what remotely credible story could he make up when he'd needed only five hundred late this afternoon? Not that he'd lost another thousand gambling—if she did believe that, it would make her so mad she'd be more likely to walk out on him than meekly agree to borrow that much on the policy for him. And she probably wouldn't believe him to begin with, and he couldn't blame her; he'd never gambled for stakes like that before, a grand in one evening. The four-eighty to Amico had been lost in his bad-luck run over several weeks.

But there had to be *some* way out. There *had* to be.

He'd walked two blocks before he decided that walking wasn't doing him any good. His mind was going in circles, getting nowhere. He could think better sitting down. And besides, the shock of Mack Irby had knocked off his slight edge, had knocked all the alcohol out of him. And he could think better with a slight edge, just a slight one, than cold sober. He needed a drink and needed it badly.

The Palace Bar was coming up. It was a place he ordinarily didn't like and seldom drank at, especially since he'd never been able to get the place on his customer list. It was mostly a workingman's bar, doing a beer trade. But they did sell whisky, and any port in a storm. Maybe it would be a better place right now than most because he'd almost certainly not run into anybody he knew there. And he didn't want to see anybody he knew.

He played safe by looking into, the window first. There were a few men in the place, mostly down at the far end of the bar, but they were all strangers. Still better, he didn't even know the bartender. Kowalsky, who ran the place, wasn't there himself and the bartender must be a new man he'd put on recently.

Ray Fleck went in and took a stool at the corner of the bar, facing the back. The bartender came over and he ordered a double, a highball. It came and he paid for it.

He sipped at it and tried to think, but nothing came, nothing constructive. He thought, damn Amico; if Amico hadn't put the heat on him, if Amico hadn't been so tough, he'd still be all right; he'd have got Amico paid off sooner or later and he wouldn't have been tempted to steal Dolly's stuff. And damn Dolly and double damn Irby; he hadn't had time to get to her place yet, but soon they'd be celebrating his check and confession and laughing at him. And then going to bed together to celebrate some more. Irby hadn't fooled him by calling his client *Miss Mason;* he was one of her men all right, and probably her steady. He wondered how many other shakedown rackets they'd worked together.

Most of all, damn Ruth. It all had started by her being selfish and unreasonable this afternoon, refusing him the five hundred he'd needed then. If she'd been reasonable and sensible then, none of the rest would have happened, none of it.

Irby had said facetiously "sell your wife." God, if only he *could* sell her. What a mistake it had been for him ever to have married in the first place. A sudden thought came to him: that damn Greek she worked for was soft on her. Maybe—No, it wouldn't work; Mikos wouldn't lend him money, soft on Ruth or not. Mikos would want him to get into trouble, bad enough trouble so Ruth would leave him and give Mikos a free field with her.

But there *had* to be an answer.

He stared down into his highball, looking for one.

11:16 P.M.

This is the transcript of a conversation that might possibly have happened. If you believe in such things you'll come to see that it could have happened. If you do not believe, it doesn't matter.

"He is set up, Sire. Everything is ready when you say the word."

"You're sure he is sufficiently frightened, sufficiently desperate and unhinged?"

"Yes, Sire."

"Ready for murder? Remember, he has committed every other sin, but he has not ever thought of murder. Not seriously, that is."

"Only because, Sire, he has known that he could not get away with it. Now we present him with the perfect opportunity. A chance to kill his wife in such a way that it cannot possibly be pinned on him. A method by which, if he alibis himself as he will, will not even cause him to be suspected."

"We can make sure by adding a little touch or two to what he thinks is his string of bad luck."

"It is unnecessary, Sire. And it would disturb the timing, which is very delicate. We would have to rearrange much."

"Very well. We shall follow the original plan. Check time and start the count-down."

"Four seconds, Sire. Three. Two. One. Now."

"Let him look up from his drink an observe the demon."

In Pete Kowaisky's Palace Bar, Ray Fleck looked up from his drink. And saw the psychopath.

11:17 P.M.

Avaunt, ye demons, and away with imaginary conversations. Let us to a very real, if suddenly conceived, plot for murder.

In Pete Kowaisky's Palace Bar, Ray Fleck looked up from his drink, in which he had found no answer to his problem, and saw the answer walking toward him.

That is, he saw a man walking toward him from the back end of the tavern, undoubtedly coming from the john; he must have been in it when Ray had come in the place a minute or so ago. Ray didn't know the man, but still he looked vaguely familiar. He was medium in height and stocky, probably about Ray's own weight except that he had broad shoulders and a narrow waist, just the opposite of Ray's distribution of weight. He had a somewhat coarse, brutal face—anyway a face that looked as though it could look brutal. And dark intense eyes that looked—well, haunted was probably the best word. For some reason he couldn't name a cold chill went down Ray Fleck's spine. He'd seen that man *somewhere* before. Where?

The man hadn't noticed Ray and obviously didn't know he was being watched and wondered about. He stopped behind the bar stool that was the second one down from Ray's and stood there a moment. There was an almost finished drink on the bar in front of that stool and apparently he was deciding whether to sit down again and finish it or to go on out of the tavern. The guy seemed agitated, lost in his own thoughts.

And in that moment as he stood there Ray knew why the chill had gone down his spine. For a moment the man's hands, *big* hands, flexed and unflexed—and then went rigid as though he'd suddenly realized what he was doing and had forced himself to stop. Then he slid onto the stool in front of the drink.

Now Ray knew, suddenly but beyond all doubt, where, when and under what circumstances he'd seen the man. He knew he was sitting two stools away from the psychopathic killer who was terrorizing the city. And who, according to what the squad car cops had told him in Jick's only half an hour or so ago, was on the prowl tonight and had already tried to get at two women.

His first thought was to get out of there fast and phone the police from the drugstore that was still open directly across the street. And hope the man would still be here when they came. Then he saw the dangers of that. For tonight—until they'd had time to dig into background and find evidence—it would be his word against the psycho's. And the cops would keep him for hours, questioning him—and bawling the hell out of him for not having reported what he'd seen when he'd seen it two months ago. They'd make him sound like more of a heel than a hero for reporting it now. And suppose he phoned in and the cops didn't get here in time to catch their man they'd be even tougher with him. And if the deal got in the newspapers the psycho would know there was someone around who could identify him, and he'd know who. That would be a hell of a spot to be in. And what did he have to gain? He had troubles of his own. And then the second thought came to him, full blown and foolproof. And he knew he had to do it right away before he lost his nerve. Or before the man finished his drink and left.

He took the rest of his own drink at a draught and called out, "Hey, bartender," to the bartender he didn't know. "One more double." And then casually to the man who sat almost beside him, "Have one with me, pal?"

The man shook his head. "Thanks. Gotta go."

Ray made his voice sound just a trifle thick and slurred; to play this convincingly he shouldn't seem cold sober. He said, "One for the road, then. Look, I won't want you to buy back, won't let you. I'm a liquor salesman, see, so any drink I buy anybody goes on the 'spense account. Besides, I hate to drink alone. Hey, bartender, make it two up this way."

"Okay," the man said. "Guess one more won't hurt me."

Ray pretended to look at his wrist watch. "One's about all I'll have time for myself. Got to get in an all-night poker game and it's starting about now. Say, my name's Ray Fleck—don't tell me yours 'cause I'm lousy on names and won't remember it anyway. I'll call you Bill. You married, Bill?"

The man shook his head. And the bartender came with their drinks. Ray paid him and left his wallet on top of the bar; he was going to need it in a minute.

"Well, I am," he said. "Married, I mean. Got the prettiest, sweetest little wife in town. And you know it worries me—with what's been happening—to leave her all alone, in a building all by herself, while I play all-night poker. But hell, a man's got to get out once in a while, and I think this is my lucky night."

He was thinking: it could be; it could be, if this works.

The man picked up his glass. "Thanks," he said. "Here's how."

"Bumps," Ray said. He took a pull, from his own glass.

"Yeah," he said. "All alone in the building, the whole damn building, that's what worries me a little. We live in a third floor, top floor, flat over a store, see. And the second floor flat is vacant right now; people moving in on the first of the month but that's a week yet. And she's the prettiest—Say, let me show you."

He opened a compartment of his wallet and took out two snapshots of his wife. He always carried them. Not out of sentiment but because so many other men carried pictures of their wives or kids or both and he didn't want to be left out if it came to a photo showing match. Besides, Ruth *was* damned pretty. One of the photos was a close-up and made her look sweet and tender. The other had been snapped at the beach, Ruth in a bathing suit. She'd probably have been annoyed that he carried that one and showed it to other men, who usually whistled when they saw it, but what she didn't know didn't hurt her.

He pushed the pictures over to the man and used the motion as an excuse to slide over one stool and sit next to him. "That's Ruth," he said. "Ruth Fleck, if you forgot my name. Ain't she a honey?"

"Sure is."

The man was bent over the photographs on the bar, studying them as closely as though he were nearsighted. Ray Fleck couldn't see his eyes, which was perhaps just as well; they might have unnerved him and he needed every bit of nerve and every bit of acting ability he had, to put this over.

He asked casually, "Ever eat at a restaurant called Mikos'? Out on North Broadmoor?"

The man still didn't look up. "Know where it is; I've driven past. But I never ate there. Why?"

"Just that if you had you might have seen Ruth. She's working there, just temporarily. Waitress on the evening shift till eleven thirty, gets home about midnight."

The man pushed the pictures back. He still didn't look at Ray; now he was looking at his drink, and put a hand around it, moving the glass in slow circles. "Good looking, all right. But what you worrying about? You got a chain bolt on the door, ain't you? Everybody has, somebody told me."

Suddenly Ray's mouth felt dry, and he knew he was winning. He had to wait a second to get saliva in his mouth so he could talk naturally. "Ordinary bolt, not a chain bolt. But she has to open up when I come—" He broke off and laughed suddenly.

"What the hell, I clean forgot. We got a system, Ruth and me. A code knock so she knows it's me if I get home after she does. She don't open the door otherwise. But I haven't had to use if for a few weeks and I clean forgot about it for the minute."

He took a sip of his drink and put the glass down again. "Imagine me forgetting, when we picked a code I couldn't forget. Same as our address. We live at three one two Covington Place, see, three knocks, then one, and then two. That way I don't have to yell out my name or anything and anyway somebody else could say 'It's Ray,' so that wouldn't mean anything. Say, who do you think will be playing in the series this year?"

The man shrugged. "I don't follow baseball. The game's too slow for me."

Ray nodded in agreement.

"I don't either, much," he said. "But I'd sure like to see the Yankees lose a pennant for once. Spoils baseball, same team winning every year in one league."

"Yeah," the man said. "I go along on that." He finished his drink and slid off the stool. "Well, I gotta go. Unless you'll let me buy back."

"Nope. This better be my last, if I'm gonna play poker."

"Okay, then. Thanks."

Ray didn't turn as the man walked behind and past him to the door. But after the man was outside he turned just slightly and managed to watch out of the corner of his eye, through the window, without appearing to be watching. The man crossed the street and went into the drugstore. He headed for the phone booth and started thumbing through the phone book that hung on a chain beside it.

Checking up on what Ray had told him by verifying the address in the phone book? It could be. But then the man looked up another number, thumbing to another part of the directory, and then entered the phone booth and closed the door behind him.

What call would he be making, Ray wondered. To Ray's own phone number, just to verify that no one answered there? That wouldn't prove much. Calling someone to tell them that he wouldn't be home till later? That didn't seem too likely; be probably lived alone, and besides he'd had to look up a number. He'd certainly know the number where- ever he lived.

Then Ray realized what call the man would be making. He was checking Ray's story down the line. First he'd looked up Ray's listing just to make sure of the address, then he'd looked up Mikos' restaurant and was now calling it. He'd ask for Ruth Fleck and be told—Ray glanced at his wrist watch and saw that it was eleven thirty-four—that yes, Ruth Fleck worked there and had just left to go home. Mikos would still be there to answer the phone; he knew enough about restaurant routine to know that Mikos always stayed at least a little while after Ruth left, to check the cash register, maybe put chairs on tables, do whatever else had to be done to shut up shop for the night.

He reached out a hand for his drink, and saw that the hand was shaking so badly from reaction that he put it quickly down on the bar instead. He had to get himself under control now, and stay that way. He didn't dare let himself think about what was going to happen to Ruth.

The die was cast now, and there was no way he could call back what he had done. All that remained was to sit there until he was calm again, and think things out. He needed an alibi.

Ruth would die any time after midnight. And so, from midnight on, he had to have a solid, airtight, unbreakable alibi. One with lots of witnesses. With a ten-thousand-dollar motive for killing his wife, the police would be utter fools if they didn't at least slightly suspect him of having done the murder himself, using the psycho's *modus operandi*—knockout, rape, strangling, in that order—and so his alibi had to be above suspicion. Already he knew approximately how he was going to work it, but there were still a few details to think out.

And his nerves. But they'd be all right; they were probably all right right now. He lifted his hand from the bar and reached for his drink. It still trembled a little, but not so badly. In a few more minutes he'd be completely okay.

If he could keep himself from thinking about Ruth.

11:34 P.M.

Ruth Fleck had not yet left the restaurant. George had told her to go at eleven thirty, but the last customer, at the counter, had obviously been within a minute or two of finishing and she'd decided to wait. It had paid off, too, with a two-bit tip that he probably wouldn't have left if he'd seen her leave; he wouldn't have known that George would hold the tip for her and give it to her tomorrow evening.

She'd carried his dishes back and was putting on the light summer coat over her uniform dress when she heard the phone ring up front. She didn't hurry because George was up there starting to check the cash register, and anyway the call was unlikely to be for her. Nobody she knew would be calling her at this hour except possibly Ray—and if he looked at his watch before calling he'd think that she'd already left.

But George's voice called out "Ruth. For you." And she called back "Coming" and hurried a bit.

George was back at the register when she came through the swinging doors, and the wall phone was off the hook, dangling on its cord. She went to it and said, "Hello." But no voice answered and after a second she realized that the faint buzz she heard was a dial tone.

She hung up the phone and looked toward George. "That's funny," she said. "Nobody on the line. It must have been Ray, but he must have been cut off. Maybe I should wait around a few more minutes to see if he tries again."

There was suddenly a peculiar expression on George Mikos' face. He left the register and came around the counter. He wiped his hands clean with a rag cut from and old table cloth and then slung it over his shoulder with a snap.

"That wasn't your husband," he said. "He's called often enough for me to know his voice. This voice was deeper. But I think you better wait a minute anyway. Sit down."

Ruth was puzzled but she pulled a chair out from under the nearest table and sat. George sat on one of the counter stools and stared at her. "Ruth, outside of Ray, do you know anyone at all who might have any reason at all for calling you at this time?"

Ruth thought, and shook her head slowly. "No," she admitted. "No man, anyway. Just what did he say? Could he have got the wrong number and you misunderstood the name he asked for."

"No. And the conversation was so short I can give it to you verbatim. He said, 'Is Ruth Fleck there?' Incidentally, that's proof, besides the voice, that it wasn't your husband. The several times he's called when I've answered he's always said, 'Hi, George. Can I talk to Ruth?' Knows my voice and calls me by name, and never bothers adding the Fleck to yours.

"But back to this call. I said, 'She's just about to leave, but she's still here. Just a minute.' And then I called out to you, and went back to the register. And that's all."

"He couldn't have misunderstood you and thought you said I'd just left?"

"Pretty unlikely, Ruth. My diction is at least passable, and it was a good connection. Besides, although my mouth was away from the mouthpiece when I called you I called loudly enough and was still close enough that he'd surely have heard that."

He frowned. "Have you had any other mysterious phone calls recently? Such as answering the phone and having someone hang up when he hears your voice?" Ruth shook her head. "Or such as wrong numbers? Or a call from a stranger who could be a phony for all you know, asking what television program you're watching, or anything like that?"

Ruth shook her head more slowly this time. "No, George. Oh, wrong numbers once in a while, things like that. But not recently. Not that I remember right now, anyway. Most calls we get are for Ray, and the caller always leaves a name or a number or both. Or if they're for me, they're from someone I know."

"And you've never been followed that you know of? Never had anything happen to indicate that someone has been checking up on you or asking questions about you?"

"No. George, you're taking this awfully seriously. I can guess what you're thinking—but why would the psychopath pick on *me?*"

"For the same reason," George said, "that he picked on, those other women. Doubled in spades, because you're prettier than they were. And you've got a husband who—What time does Ray usually come home at night?"

"Usually about ten or fifteen minutes after the taverns close at one o'clock. I always stay up that long to wait for him. If he isn't home by—oh, about one twenty—I figure he probably got into a poker game or something and go to sleep. Then he has to knock loud enough to wake me—but that's not too hard; I'm a light sleeper."

"That would give the psycho a full hour, from midnight till one, most nights. Some nights longer, if he's been casing your husband too and happens to know he's going to be later. Ruth, I don't like that phone call at all. To be honest about it, it worries the bejesus out of me."

"You're scaring me too, George. I guess you want to, so I'll be careful. And I will. I told you about the special knock Ray uses when he gets home late. I wouldn't open the door except to that knock. But isn't it enough of a precaution?"

"I suppose so, unless Ray's told someone about it. Suppose he got talking to a friend in a tavern—but with the psycho in hearing distance—and told him about it. There's plenty of talk about the psycho, including in taverns. If the subject came up naturally, mightn't he tell what precaution you and he are using, if he knew and thought he could trust whoever he was talking to."

"Well—he might mention that we use a code knock. But he surely wouldn't tell just what the code knock *is.* There'd be no reason for him to tell that—unless he deliberately wanted to get me murdered. And he's not that bad, George."

George Mikos sighed. "I suppose you're right there. But don't you see that, code knock or no, you can be in danger? That you *are* in danger if friend psycho is checking up on you and has you on his little list, even as a possibility?"

"I realize that—but still, if I don't open the door—"

"Wait, I hadn't finished. If he's even intelligent enough to read the newspapers he knows by now that women alone just aren't opening doors these days, not unless they have chain bolts on them anyway. He knows he's going to have to vary his procedure if he's going to succeed again. And what simpler variation would there be than for him to find a woman who went home alone, late, and be waiting for her *inside* her house or flat when she gets there?

"Let me make a hypothetical case to show you how that could be. Let's say he picked you out a week ago. Maybe he eats here; maybe you've talked to him and he got to know your name. Let's say the first night he followed you home and knows where you live.

"Let's say he's been checking up on you ever since then. It wouldn't be hard for him to learn that you're married, but only you and your husband live in that flat."

"Only Ray and I live in the whole building right now, George. It's a small, narrow building, two flats over a hardware store. And the flat on the second floor, under us, is vacant. I understand it's been rented for the first, and we'll have neighbors soon, but—"

"That makes it a perfect setup for him, Ruth. Better than he could have hoped for. He wouldn't have to come in the restaurant here again, or follow you home again. Let's say he's just been keeping an eye on your building late evenings and nights since. He's seen you get home about midnight every night. And he's seen Ray—How long has it been since Ray has got home early, before a few minutes after one?"

"Not for over a week."

"All right. Then he knows you get home at midnight, and Ray doesn't get home until after one. Since there are only two of you in the whole building he wouldn't have to know Ray even by sight to know that the man who came in an hour or more after you got home is your husband. He wouldn't have to know a thing about Ray except that he gets home after one. He probably figures Ray holds a night job somewhere and that's when he gets off, so he's even surer than he should be that Ray isn't going to get home earlier. Are you following me, Ruth?"

"I'm getting plenty scared, if that's what you mean."

"So he knows he's got an hour with you there alone, and that's probably a lot more time than he needs. His attacks are probably as quick as they are sudden and brutal.

"So all he has to do is break into your flat any time before midnight and wait for you. Break in or let himself in with a skeleton key or something. How good is your lock?"

"Just an ordinary one. And of course the bolt isn't thrown inside the door when no one's there. I guess a skeleton key would get him in."

"He could be there right now waiting for you. And that call for you here—he could have made it right from your phone, just to assure himself that you were getting off on time and not working late. He must have expected me to say that you'd just left, and when I said you were still here he couldn't think quickly enough of anything unsuspicious to say to you so he hung up before you got to the phone. And he did learn that you'll be there soon; I gave him that information gratuitously when I told him you were still here but just about to leave."

"George, this is—horrible. It's an awful lot to build on one unexplained phone call but—but it could be. Do you think we should go to the police?"

He shook his head slowly. "Not tonight. I'm afraid they'd think, as you suggested, that it's an awful lot to build on one unexplained phone call. They might think it worth investigating and they might not. In any case, they'd want to talk to us first, maybe have us come in, and that would waste a lot of time. And don't forget that if he *is* there waiting for you, he isn't going to wait forever. If you're not home by—oh, say, half past twelve, he'll figure something's gone wrong and beat it.

"No, I'm going to handle it myself, tonight. I'm going to drive you home. You're going to give me your key and then wait in the car till I go up and check your flat. Thoroughly. You go up only when I tell you it's safe as houses. And then lock yourself in and don't open the door till your husband uses his trick knock. And bolt the door again after him. That way you'll be safe for tonight.

"And we'll worry about the police tomorrow—unless by then we've found some explanation of that phone call—and I'll go right to my homicide captain friend and lay it in his lap. If he takes this as seriously as I do you'll be under police protection from then on. I'd call him tonight but I happen to know he's out of town till tomorrow morning. And I don't want to mess with any lesser lights. Come on."

He stood up and went to the front door to double check that it was locked. "My car's out back. We'll go that way."

Ruth had stood but she said, "George—I don't like this. Your going up there alone, I mean. If he's *there,* he's dangerous. You don't know how big and strong he may be."

He grinned. "I know how big and strong *I* am. And clothed in armor of righteousness at that. Believe me, nothing would make me happier than finding him."

"But—he might be armed. Do you have a gun?"

"He probably isn't. People who kill with their hands seldom carry other weapons. But yes, I've got a gun, back in the sanctum. I'll take it along if only to make you feel easier. And a flashlight to help me find wall switches and look under beds. Come on."

This time she followed him and waited in the kitchen while he went briefly into his office. They turned out rest of the lights and left.

In the car, which was parked on a vacant lot across the alley, he gave him the address and directions, since he'll never been there before. It was only five minutes by car, she thought; she'd be getting home earlier than usual instead of later. The bus took half an hour because it was roundabout and she had to transfer once.

She had a thought, as he started. "George, what if Ray came home early and is there? What are you going to tell him?"

"The truth, what else? And he'll have no cause for suspicion, if that's what you're worrying about. If I were taking you there for an assignation I'd hardly leave you in the car and go up alone, would I? Besides, next to the psycho I'd *like* to find him there. I'd feel safer about leaving you. And there's a possibility, just a possibility, that he could tell us something about that mysterious phone call. For some reason or another he might have asked or told someone to call you. And the hanging up *could* have been a misunderstanding or an accidental disconnection. Why did you ask? He isn't jealous of me, is he?"

"I've never given him any cause to be. I mean, I haven't talked about you too much or anything like that. He knows I think you're nice, and generous, and a good employer."

"Uh-huh. Do you have any reason for thinking he might come home earlier than usual tonight? Or, for that matter, later?"

"Well, there could be—either way. I told you about our quarrel this afternoon because I wouldn't borrow money against the policy for him. It was pretty bitter. He might deliberately stay out later because of that, if he's still mad. Or he might come home early or be there already for the opposite reason, I mean if he's repentant or wants to apologize. But I doubt that. If he *is* home early it's more likely to reopen the argument and have another try at convincing me. Or— This is Thursday, isn't it?"

"Yes. What's that got to do with it?"

"Only that quite frequently he plays poker Thursday nights, all night or quite late. But he probably won't play tonight—he didn't have too much money and I guess it's a pretty steep game, one he wouldn't try to get into with a few dollars."

"He might have borrowed some. But skip Ray. Tell me something about the flat I'll be casing in a minute. Has it got a fire escape, could it be broken into from the outside?"

"No fire escape. There's a front and back door. The back door leads to stairs that go down to the alley. But it's kept bolted and I never use it except to take down garbage or trash. I won't do that tonight."

"Nor tomorrow either. You're going to be extra careful in all directions at least until I've had a talk with my friend in homicide and see what we can work out with him. He'll know what to do. How many windows?"

"Five—no, six. Two at the front that look on the street, three along one side and one kitchen window at the back. But he couldn't get at any of them without using a long ladder, and I can't picture him taking the risk of carrying one around."

George said, "Just the same I'm going to see that all windows are closed and locked when I go up there. It's a coolish night and you can survive without ventilation for that long. How about access to or from the roof?"

"There's a trap door, but it's outside the kitchen door; if he came through it he still wouldn't be inside the flat. Besides, it's kept fastened on the inside."

"This the right block?"

"Yes. Third building from the next corner, on your right." She started fishing in her handbag for her key and had it ready for him by the time the car stopped directly in front.

He got out and closed the door, spoke through the open window. "Don't leave the car. If he's by any chance watching from somewhere and approaches the car—if *anyone* approaches the car—start yelling like hell, loud enough for me to hear you up there. Not that your yelling wouldn't make him run in any case."

He left her and Ruth Fleck lighted a cigarette and waited till he came back. This time he came to her side of the car and opened the door for her. "False alarm." he said cheerfully. "Not a psycho in sight—and I checked carefully. Closets, under the bed, anywhere a man could hide."

She got out of the car. "Thanks, George. I can't tell you how much I—"

"Don't try then. And I'm not leaving you this second anyway. Escort service right to your door, and I want to hear the bolt slide when you've closed it after you. Here's your key."

He stopped at the door of the flat and didn't try to enter after her. She turned to face him. "Good night, George. And thanks again, a million."

"Forget it. But listen a moment. My guess that he might be waiting here for you was wrong, but I'm still worried and I guess you are too. Would you feel safer spending the night in a hotel room? You could write a note for Ray—I'd have had to bring you here to do that in any case—and then I could drive you on downtown. It might be the safest thing." She shook her head. "No, I'll be all right here."

"Okay. But one final instruction—and I don't mean not to open the door except for your husband; you know that. It's this: if you hear anyone trying to get in either door or at a window, if you even *think* you hear anything suspicious, don't waste time phoning the police—you could be dead by the time they get here. Just open a front window, lean out and start screaming bloody murder at the top of your lungs, loud enough to carry six blocks away. He wouldn't follow through on trying to get in while you're doing that. Okay, good night—and let me hear that bolt slide."

"Good night, George."

She closed the door and slid the bolt, stood there a moment listening to his footsteps going down the stairs and thinking how wonderful, he'd been to her and how concerned he'd been about her. And how brave to have come up here alone when he'd really thought that a dangerous criminal, a murderer, might be waiting.

When she turned she saw by the clock that it still lacked six minutes of midnight. Because of the lift, she was home earlier than usual despite all the talking they'd done and the time George had taken to search the flat.

She went into the bathroom and started drawing water in the tub. She was tired, if not sleepy, and a hot bath would be just the thing to relax her body and her nerves.

11:55 P.M.

Ray Fleck looked at his watch again and saw that it was just time for him to leave. He'd sat there nursing his drink ever since the psycho had left—thinking. There couldn't be any possible slip-ups on his alibi and he'd thought it out and covered every contingency.

The all-night poker game at Harry Brambaugh's was, of course, the basis of it. But he'd worked things out so that game would alibi him for all night no matter what happened. Someone in the game might or might not buy the diamond ring to let him play. And if someone did buy it, he might still go broke within the first hour, and that would be no good at all. His alibi had to be for *all* night, clear up to dawn.

He'd told the psycho, in effect, that an attack on Ruth would be safe any time after midnight; he couldn't possibly pinpoint it by suggesting a specific time or even a deadline. And for all Ray knew the guy might as easily make his call at two or three in the morning as at half past twelve. Besides, even if he had any way of timing it, he didn't dare get home too soon after the psycho had left. The minute he got home and found Ruth dead he'd have to call the police—and if she were freshly dead they'd still suspect him of having killed her and having done it in such a way as to throw suspicion on the psycho. He didn't dare find her until she'd been dead at least a couple of hours, and with him having a solid alibi for the time at which she'd died.

To be safe he didn't dare get home before five in the morning and six would be better.

So, since the psycho had left, he'd been planning carefully; he was going to have an all-night alibi from Harry and whoever else was in the game, whether or not he could sell the ring and whether or not he went broke quickly if he did sell it. All it took was the right build-up.

Harry had a downtown apartment, only a block and a half from here. Five minutes walk and if he left at five of twelve he could establish the time of his arrival by saying "Cold on the stroke of midnight," when he walked into the room. That wouldn't sound suspicious or as though he was trying to establish an alibi because it was a phrase he often used anyway. So did some of the other boys. It was a quotation from a poem or something, and it was a cliché that fitted in any time the question of time came up at or within a minute of midnight.

Second step: The minute he got in he'd tell Harry he felt lousy, had an upset stomach and a headache. He'd say it would probably wear off, but did Harry have a Bromo-Seltzer or an Alka-Seltzer around, and maybe a couple of aspirin tablets too. And Harry would have; Harry had a bad stomach and headaches himself and was always well stocked with patent medicines; Harry would give him something and he'd take it. Point made.

Then, at the poker table but before sitting down, he'd explain apologetically that he was short on cash but had a hell of a bargain in a diamond ring, if anyone might be interested in buying it, and he'd pass it around. He'd try to get a hundred, but settle for fifty if someone wanted it but quibbled about price. Either someone would buy it or no one would buy it.

If no one bought, well, he'd laid his groundwork, by convincing Harry he was sick. He'd say he didn't feel up to going home right away, and would Harry mind if he lay down on the sofa a while first. Harry had a comfortable sofa right in the living room, the room in which they played cards. Lying there he'd be in sight of everyone in the game. And Harry was a nice guy; he certainly wouldn't mind. That sofa had been used before for similar purposes; once in a while someone got tired in the middle of a game and wanted to rest a while and then get back in.

So he'd pretend to go to sleep on the sofa—or really go to sleep if he could. And stay there till the game broke up, which was never before five o'clock.

Same deal with a minor variation if he sold the ring but lost the money too soon. His upset stomach and headache would have come back by then; he'd take more Alka-Seltzer and aspirin and then lie down a while to give them a chance to work.

It would work. Parts of the story might sound mildly strange to the police when they questioned him, but there'd be too many witnesses for them to have any serious, doubts. Especially if Milt Corbett was there as one of the witnesses, as he probably would be; Milt was a prominent member of the city council and the strength of his word would be as the strength of ten, to the police.

He left a dollar tip on the bar, to make the bartender remember him; it wouldn't hurt to be able to extend his alibi backward a bit in case Ruth died very shortly after midnight, and left.

He'd timed it right; it was midnight on the head when he rang the bell of Harry Brambaugh's apartment.

Stella, Brambaugh's wife, opened the door. On a chain, of course, but she opened it the rest of the way when she recognized Ray. He was a little surprised to see that she was wearing a robe and had her iron gray hair in pin curlers; usually she stayed dressed and made coffee and sandwiches about one o'clock, and then went to bed.

"Cold on the stroke of midnight," Ray said. "Game been going on long?"

"Ray, I tried to call you but you weren't home. There isn't any game. Harry got a telegram while we were eating tonight; his brother is seriously hurt in a car accident and he had to leave right away, the first plane. He gave me a list of six men to call up, and I got all of them except you."

Ray frowned, thinking frantically. "Mrs. Brambaugh, I wonder if you could give me that list. I know all the boys on it, but not all their phone numbers. And maybe we can still get a game going, especially if you'd let me use your phone so I can call them right away."

She shook her head. "I might find the list in the wastebasket, but it wouldn't work anyway, Ray. Three of them said they wouldn't have been able to make it tonight anyway. I don't know whether Harry would have played four-handed or not; he'd probably have postponed it. But that leaves only two besides yourself, and they've probably got doing something else by now. Or gone to bed."

His mind went in frantic circles as he walked down the stairs and out into the night. What now? He could alibi himself by going to any tavern where he was well known, between now and one o'clock when the tavern would close. God, oh, God, what could he do? He could go to a hotel, but what good would that be as an alibi? The clerk could testify when he checked in and when he checked out, but could he give positive testimony that he had not sneaked out and back in again sometime during the night?

Of course if he picked up a woman and took her to a hotel, or to her own place— He considered that and abandoned it reluctantly. The testimony of a woman like that would be of only slight value, for one thing. For another, the chances of his finding such a woman were slight, especially since he had less than an hour to do it in. There'd been a recent crackdown and available pickups in bars were currently few and far between. Outside of bars, he didn't have the faintest idea where to start looking. He didn't have a little black book of addresses; for the last few years, his only extramarital adventures had been those with Dolly, and Dolly—well, he could forget Dolly tonight, if not forever.

Besides, he was broke. He couldn't have over a few dollars left after all the drinks, many of them doubles, that he'd been buying.

For a moment he entertained the wild idea of walking in front of a car, getting himself injured and taken to the hospital. But that was too risky; he could be killed—or permanently crippled, which would be almost as bad. Or if for safety he picked a slowly moving car and just let it knock him down his injuries would probably be so superficial that a hospital would simply check him over and discharge him immediately. Could he feign a heart attack? No, it would take the admitting physician only half a minute with a stethoscope to learn that his heart was as sound as a pre-inflation dollar. Acute appendicitis? Hardly, with his appendix already out and a scar to prove it. Or—no, damn it, he knew too little about illnesses to be able to get away with feigning anything. He'd never had a sick day in his life, except for that attack of appendicitis and the time he'd been in the army infirmary on account of his allergy to wool.

The hospital idea wouldn't work. But what else would be open all night after the taverns closed?

The answer was so simple that he wondered why he'd sweated thinking about hotels and hospitals. The jail was open all night. It wouldn't hurt him to spend a night in the drunk tank, to save his life, and to pay a ten-buck fine in the morning. Maybe even no fine, just a warning, for first offense; and what alibi could possible be better than being in jail? He wondered why he hadn't thought of it the moment he'd learned that the poker game was called off.

But he'd better make it good and *really* get drunk, roaring drunk, not depend on acting. He looked at his watch. It was only five minutes after twelve. Fifty-five minutes to go and that was plenty of time, if he drank straight shots, doubles. He had a hell of a good capacity for liquor if he took it in highballs and reasonably spaced his drinks—as he had thus far tonight—but straight whisky always hit him hard and fast. With the slight edge he already had, five or six straight doubles would be plenty, if he took them no more than five minutes apart. He regretted having the steak for dinner. An empty stomach would be better.

Money wouldn't be a problem, even though he had only two bucks, enough for two doubles, left. Since he'd never done so before, he could borrow five or ten from almost any bar owner or bartender in town. And even five, with what he had, would get him seven doubles, more than enough. He'd been walking without thinking where he was going, but now he looked to see where he was. Half a block from the Log Cabin, run by Jerry Dean. It would be as good a place as any. He was known there at least as well as at any other tavern, and Jerry was at least as likely to lend him money as anyone else; he'd spent hundreds of dollars in Jerry's.

Jerry was behind the bar and, Ray was glad to see, so was his son Shorty Dean, whom Jerry was teaching to be a bartender. Two witnesses would be better than one—and he might as well establish the time right away. He put a dollar on the bar and asked for a straight double. Then while Jerry was pouring it he glanced up at the wall clock. "Hey, your clock's half an hour off."

Jerry looked up at the clock and then at his own watch. "Seven after twelve. That's what I got. How about you, Shorty?"

Shorty had five after, but said his watch had been running a minute or two slow a day.

"Then seven after must be right," Ray said. He held his own watch to his ear. "Hell, mine's stopped. Must have forgot to wind it." He wound it and pretended to set it. "Say, Jerry, I ran short of cash tonight. Can you spare a sawbuck, just till tomorrow night?"

"Sure, Ray." Jerry pulled out a wallet. "Can even make it a double-saw, if you want."

"Swell," Ray said. He left the bill on the bar and tossed off his double. It tasted like hell to him; he didn't like the taste of raw whisky. But he ordered another.

Twenty minutes and four drinks later he was feeling high, definitely high. His tongue was thick and if he stared fixedly at anything or anybody he found himself seeing double; to keep his eyes focused he had to move them frequently. And he knew that the full force of the drinks hadn't hit him yet; fifteen minutes or half an hour more and he'd feel them a lot worse.

"One more," he said.

"Listen, Ray, you've had plenty. Don't you think you'd better call it off for tonight?" Jerry sounded genuinely concerned. "Uh—are you driving?"

"Nope. Car's being worked on. So one more, then I'll call it off. Okay?"

But he sat staring at the one more, and he was realizing that maybe getting arrested for being drunk wasn't as easy as getting drunk was. How do you get arrested if there isn't a cop around? Was he going to have to start trouble or a fight so Jerry would have to call the cops? He hated trouble, and he hated fights worse, but—

And then the answer came through the door. Officer Hoff and his squad car partner, the pair he'd talked to earlier in Jick's place, came in. Hoff said, "Hi, Jerry. Two damn quick quickies. Hi, Ray. How goes it?"

This was his chance. With drunken dignity Ray got off the stool and started back toward the juke box. He tried to stagger— and found that he didn't have to try. He almost fell, caught himself with a hand against the wall, and apparently forgot where he'd been going and came back to his stool, but stood there behind it, swaying. He reached for his drink and spilled half of it, got the rest down and dropped the glass. He swayed back onto the stool—he was exaggerating, acting, but not much—and sat there glowering at Hoff. "Goddam cop," he said thickly. "God, how I hate cops."

"Look, Hoffie," Jerry said in a conciliatory tone, "he's drunk, so don't get mad. And don't blame me. This hit him sudden like, or I'd of cut him off sooner. He's been in here only twenty minutes or so, and he acted cold sober till just now. I'd hate to see him get jugged—Ray's a nice guy. Could you guys spare time to run him home and get him out of trouble?"

Hoff said, "Sure, Jerry. Ray's all right. It can happen to any of us." He downed his shot quickly and then came back and put his hand on Ray's arm. "Come on, Ray. Time for beddy-bye. Where do you live?"

Ray slid off the stool and jerked away. If only violence was going to get him arrested, then he might as well get it over with. "Keep your goddam hands off me. Mind your own damn business." And he started a roundhouse swing. He didn't really know whether or not he was trying to make it connect—but it didn't. And then he saw Hoff's fist coming up in a short sharp uppercut for his own chin—saw it, but not in time to duck. The lights went out.

He came to, to the sound and motion of a car. Thank God, it had worked; they were taking him in. He shook his head to clear it a little and saw that Hoff was sitting beside him in the back seat, the partner was driving.

Hoff said, "Take it easy, Ray. I can handle you but I don't want to have to hurt you. And you're not pinched—this time. I got your address from your wallet—and put your money that was on the bar in it. We're taking you home to the little wifie."

Oh, God, Oh, God, he thought; *this can't be happening. They can't take me home now. It's only half past twelve or a few minutes later. It's too early, it's hours too early.*

Under an alcoholic haze, part of his mind worked; it scuttled like a rat trying to get out of a trap. And it found a hole—a dangerous hole, but still a hole.

He reached into his left pants pocket and pulled out a handkerchief, unfolded it. As they passed a street light, jewels flashed. "Lookit, Hoffie," Ray said. "Why I was getting drunk. Stole this. Conscience. Give m'self up."

Hoff called out, "Hey, Willie. Pull in to the curb and give me the dome light on."

On the way back downtown, the way toward the police station, Hoff kept questioning him and he kept ducking. Yeah, he'd stolen the jewels. Didn't remember who from. Drunk. Needed sleep, let him tell 'em everything tomorrow when he'd sobered up.

He played drunker than he was and he was thinking that he hadn't really given anything away. Tomorrow he could deny everything. He could say he'd found the jewelry, in a hand-kerchief just as it was, and how could they prove he hadn't? They'd doubt him, but they couldn't prove a thing. Dolly and Irby weren't reporting the robbery, now that they had the check and confession, so there'd be no theft report to match the stuff. Why then had he told Hoff he'd stolen it? How did he know why? He was drunk, didn't remember anything after taking a swing at Hoff in Jerry's place. Some drunken impulse must have made him tell Hoff that, but he couldn't remember what it was, couldn't even remember having been in a squad car.

He was safe. They might doubt him, but they couldn't prove a thing, except the drunk and disorderly charge—and they certainly wouldn't press even that after they had to tell him that his wife had been knifed during the night, by the psycho. And on that angle, he was even safer; his alibi was solid from seven minutes after twelve on. From midnight on, really; Stella Brambaugh could testify she'd talked to him cold on the stroke of midnight, and just seven minutes away from Jerry's Log Cabin. Even farther back than that if the dollar tip had made the bartender at the Palace Bar remember him, and remember what times he'd been there. But even midnight was safe enough; Ruth didn't even get home until then.

Hoff said, "Ray, we've got to take you in. Want me to phone your wife so she'll know where you are?"

"God no," Ray said, and then made his voice calmer. "She won't worry about me—thinks I'm in an all-night poker game so won't 'spect me home anyhow."

"Okay. We're going to have to book you on suspicion of theft. Want a lawyer? He might get you out on bail right away."

"Hell no, Hoffie. Too drunk to do any good if I did get out. Too drunk, too sleepy. Just book me and jug me, and let me get some sleep."

"If that's the way you want it," Hoff said. The squad car pulled up in front of the station.

1:01 A.M.

Bare feet tucked under her, Ruth Fleck sat on the sofa in the living room. After her leisurely bath she'd put on pajamas and a quilted housecoat, but no slippers; she liked to go barefoot around the house. The reading lamp was on and she had a magazine in her lap, opened to the beginning of a story. But she hadn't started it yet; she was still thinking about her coming conversation with Ray.

Not about what she was going to say; she'd already decided that, but about how she was going to say it. She was going to give him an ultimatum, but to spare his pride as well as to avoid another argument, she wanted to figure how to word it so it wouldn't sound like an ultimatum.

She'd thought about it all evening at work and had finally, if a bit reluctantly, decided to give him the five hundred he needed to pay off his bookie. George was probably right in saying that Joe Amico wouldn't have him beaten up, let alone taken for a ride. But still, Ray *was* in trouble, with that big a debt hanging over him and she should help him out, this once. She'd agree to go downtown with him tomorrow and arrange the loan against the policy.

But she was going to attach a condition to it, and she thought she had every right to do so. He'd have to promise, and mean the promise and stick to it, to quit gambling on credit—or for heavy stakes, whether on credit or not. Gambling was in his blood, and she knew it would be meaningless for her to demand his promise never to gamble again. He might make such a promise—for the sake of getting the money from her—but he wouldn't mean it in the slightest and wouldn't keep it for a single day. She might as well make a clean break with him right now as to demand a promise like that.

Would she be better off in any case to make a clean break? She pushed that thought away. She should give him one more chance before she decided anything like that. And maybe the sweating he was doing right now about that five-hundred-dollar debt had taught him the lesson he needed. She'd see.

She'd give him the money—and the ultimatum. Henceforth his gambling had to be moderate and for cash only, when he could afford it. If he wanted to make two-dollar bets, or even an occasional five or ten-dollar bet, for cash, that was all right. But no more going in over his head on credit. Certainly that was a reasonable thing for a wife to expect.

But if he ever got into trouble like this again—well, again she'd borrow five hundred against the policy (that would still leave nine thousand coming, a nice nest egg, when the policy matured in another five years or so) but she wouldn't give it to Ray to pay off gambling debts. She'd use it herself for a trip to Reno. That was just about what such a trip, and a divorce, would cost her. Less than that, of course, if she could find work there during her waiting period, but she wouldn't count on that. A lot of women who go there for divorces must look for work to help out and to occupy their time during the six weeks—she thought it was six weeks—they had to wait for their divorces. The labor market might be glutted.

She hoped he wouldn't be late tonight—but no matter how late he might be, she was going to wait up for him. Morning was a bad time to talk with him, especially about anything serious. He was always irritable and grumpy in the morning, likely to fly off the handle over even the most innocent remark she might make.

She heard footsteps coming up the stairs and thought *Good, he's even a little earlier than usual.* It was only a few minutes after one; he couldn't have waited even till the bars closed to start home. Maybe that was a good sign.

She got off the sofa and went to the door. But, remembering the phone call and George's warning, she didn't reach for the bolt or the knob until he knocked.

He knocked. Three knocks, a short pause; one knock, a short pause, then two knocks.

She threw back the bolt and opened the door.

1:05 A.M.

Silently screaming, Benny Knox awakened from the nightmare. Occasionally, not too often, he had nightmares but this
one was the worst ever.

It was a hell of a nightmare, quite literally. He'd been in hell,
the very literal hell that his father had talked about so often,
either to him alone or in sermons that Benny had heard. He was
stark naked and standing knee deep in a lake of boiling, bubbling
pitch. His feet and legs hurt horribly.

At the edge of the lake, a few feet away, stood three devils.
Bright red devils with tails and horns and hoofs. Two of them
had long pitchforks and they were jabbing them into Benny's
chest and stomach, to drive him farther and deeper into the
boiling lake. His arms were stuck; he couldn't use them to try to
ward off the pitchforks. The pitchforks hurt badly and he was
forced to take a step backward and was suddenly in the boiling
pitch up almost to his waist. The slope was steep, and with
another step or two he'd be completely in the lake.

The other devil, the one in the middle, didn't have a pitch
fork. He was just standing there laughing. And even through his
dream Benny knew that he had heard that exact laugh before and
that he'd seen that devil's face before—but he couldn't remember
where or when. Over the laughter and from somewhere overhead,
came a Voice. The voice of God or the voice of his father; he
didn't know which.

"Hell forever, my son, for you have done evil. You can be
forgiven only if you can make *them* believe you, and be punished
on Earth for the evil you have done."

He tried to scream and answer but his voice was stuck too, like
his arms. Then one of the pitchforks jabbed at his eyes and he

had to take another step backward. He lost his balance and fell. As the boiling pitch closed over his head, he awoke.

Or had it been just a dream? Might not it have been a vision sent him by God or by his father in Heaven, to warn him, to instruct him?

He lay there sweating in the upper bunk, and then he remembered what Mrs. Saddler had told him to do whenever he awakened from a nightmare: get up and walk, walk till you're wide awake again and the nightmare goes away.

He climbed down from the upper bunk and walked—as far as he could in the cell, three paces one way and three back and three paces one way and three paces back— But the dream, if it had been a dream, stayed with him, more vivid than any of his memories of anything else that had happened to him that day or recently.

A sound made him pause in his pacing and look into the lower bunk. The sound was a snore. He saw that he was no longer alone in the cell; while he'd slept they'd put someone else there and he was now lying in the lower bunk. Fully dressed, as Benny was, except for shoes and coat. Even in the dim light of the cell, the man looked familiar to him.

Benny bent over him.

It was Mister Fleck. That surprised him, but what surprised him a thousand times more was that it was also the devil in his nightmare or vision, the devil without a pitchfork, the one who had laughed at him. The face of Mr. Fleck and of that devil were the same. And he remembered now why the laugh of that devil had sounded as though he'd heard it before. It was Mister Fleck's laugh, as Mister Fleck had laughed at him early in the evening, when he'd told Mister Fleck that he'd killed those women. The police hadn't *believed* him, but they hadn't laughed at him.

And suddenly he knew what he had to do to make the police really believe him, to make them believe that he'd done evil and must be punished.

He put his hands on Mister Fleck's shoulders and pulled him up to a sitting position. "Mister Fleck!" he said.

Mister Fleck's eyes opened and blinked. "Huh?" he said.

Benny was very earnest because this was very serious. "Listen, Mister Fleck," he said. "I'm sorry, but I got to kill you. I got to kill you like I killed them women so the police will believe I killed them."

"Huh? Benny—?"

"I want you to know, Mister Fleck, I ain't mad at you. Even if you laughed at me. It's bad to kill because you're mad and I want you to know I ain't mad. I just got to kill you. And besides, it won't be evil for me to kill you to make them believe me. It won't be evil, Mister Fleck, because you're a devil."

Mister Fleck opened his mouth to say something, or to scream, but nothing came out because Benny's hands were tight around his throat, and getting tighter. A minute later they let go, and something limp and dead fell back on the lower bunk.

Benny Knox went to the door of the cell and grabbed his bars, rattling the door loudly. Even more loudly he yelled, "Policemen! Policemen! Come here and see. *Now* do you believe me? *Now* will you try to tell me I never killed nobody?"

This time they believed him.

2:45 A.M.

In his office off the kitchen of the restaurant, George Mikos paced a while, too keyed up to sit down and type, which was what he'd come here to do. Finally he sat down at the desk, took the cover off the typewriter and put fresh paper into it. He began to type:

Dear Perry:

This has been the damnedest night. If you'll forgive the cliché, hell has been popping right and left.

Yes, this is a new letter and not a continuation of the one I started to you earlier. Everything has changed so completely that it would seem silly to go on with that one. But I'll enclose it, uncompleted, with this, so you'll have the background to understand what *this* one is about.

It started a few minutes after eleven thirty, when I'd just closed up and was starting to check the register. There was a phone call and a man's voice—not her husband's—asked for Ruth Fleck. She was still here, getting ready to leave. I called her to the phone but there was no one on the line when she got there.

You can deduce what I guessed from that, when she admitted she could think of no possible reason why any man except her husband should be calling her at that time of night.

I insisted on driving her home, and I also had her wait in the car while I went up and searched her flat to make sure there wasn't a reception committee waiting for her there. (I had told her I was bringing a gun so she wouldn't worry about me doing this; actually I don't even own one.) Then I escorted her upstairs, made sure she bolted herself in, and left.

But I didn't go very far. I was more worried than I let her think (luckily) and I drove off only in case she'd be watching from a front window or listening for the sound of my car starting. I U-turned at the corner and drove back the way I'd come, parked on the opposite side of the street and a quarter of a block away. I'd decided to watch the doorway of that building until I saw her husband come home, no matter how late it might be.

She had a code knock of some kind worked out with her husband so she'd know it was he when he came home and I'd impressed on her not to throw the bolt otherwise. But I was still worried about her for two reasons. First, she was confident Ray wouldn't have done any talking in bars about that code knock, but I wasn't. Second, while neither the door to her flat nor the bolt on it were flimsy, neither were they so strong that a husky, heavy man might not be able to break in with one good hard lunge. And it turned out I was right on both of those counts.

At about one o'clock I saw, or thought I saw, Ray Fleck come around the corner and go into the entrance of the building. But he'd hardly disappeared and I hadn't yet turned the ignition key in the car when I did the god damnedest double take and realized that the man I'd seen had *not* been Ray Fleck. He'd been about the same height and weight but not the same build; his bulk had been across the shoulders and he had a narrow waist, whereas Fleck's weight distribution is just the opposite.

And I was out of the car and running. If my second impression had been wrong, if it had really been Fleck I'd seen, I was about to make an awful ass of myself, but I was willing to chance that rather than to take the opposite chance. When I got to the third floor I saw the door was closed and not broken down—so I must have been right about Fleck talking; she'd never have opened the door except to that special knock. I didn't waste time trying the knob, which was just as well since the door had been bolted again from the inside; I threw my weight against the door, so hard that I still have a sore right shoulder, and the door burst open and I almost fell into the living room.

He'd heard, of course; he was in the doorway of the bedroom and rushed me before I got my balance. I managed to turn my head in time to take a vicious blow on the ear (it's still ringing) instead of the jaw. I took a couple of steps back to get on balance and then started to move in on him. I'm a wrestler; I wanted to grapple instead of trying to slug it out. He cooperated, in a way; he rushed me, head down for a solar plexus butt, both fists cocked low to start pumping into my stomach or groin as soon as he connected with the butt.

He couldn't have pleased me more. I moved just enough aside at the last split second to let his head graze past my right side and then I clamped down my arm and had a solid headlock on him. I twisted my body around and twisted his neck with it. Until there was a quite audible snap as his neck broke, and the fight was over. It had probably lasted all of three seconds.

I didn't even bother to check whether or not he was dead; if by any chance he wasn't, he wasn't going to be dangerous for a long time. I just dropped him and ran into the bedroom.

Ruth was lying on the bed, unconscious, where he'd no doubt carried her after knocking her out with a single blow as he came through the doorway.

But otherwise, I'd got there in time. She hadn't been raped, let alone strangled. Her jaw was beginning to swell but it didn't look as though it was broken—and I learned later at the hospital that it wasn't. She was breathing normally, and her heartbeat was okay.

He'd ripped open the housecoat that she was wearing, and torn the tops of her pajamas. I put a cover over her partial (and very beautiful) nakedness and then went to the living room again. I checked the psychopath to see if he was dead; he was. And then I used the phone to call for a police ambulance. The guy I got on the phone annoyingly wanted details, but I told him a woman had been injured by the psycho and I wanted the ambulance fast and I'd do all the talking they wanted after she was hospitalized. I told him they didn't have to worry about the psycho any more; they could send a meat wagon for him at their leisure. He wasn't going anywhere. Then I hung up.

And then went back to wait by Ruth, in case she should recover consciousness before the ambulance came.

But I'd sat there only a few minutes, and hadn't heard any sirens yet, when the phone rang. I answered it and—

Now hold on to your hat, Perry. Here comes the incredible part. It was the city jail, wanting Ruth Fleck. When I'd convinced them that she couldn't come to the phone but I'd take any message, I was told that I should tell her that her husband was dead. He had been killed—strangled, mind you

—by a man in the same double cell with him. Fleck had given himself up and was being held on suspicion of theft His killer was (or had been) a harmless moron who was being held overnight because he'd made a false confession of murder. He was unable to give any coherent account of why he'd killed Fleck; he talked about laughter, and devils, and the police not believing him. Although they'd known the man was slightly unbalanced mentally, he'd always been completely harmless, and they'd thought nothing of putting another prisoner in the same cell with him.

That was all l could learn; tomorrow I'll see what more I can learn, and I hope it's something that will make things make sense. I hate coincidences, and it takes a lot to make me believe in one. Especially one as extravagant as a man getting, himself strangled to death on the same night his wife would, except for my intervention, have been strangled to death—and not by the same strangler.

The man at the jail said Ray'd *given himself up*. I can't see him doing that, on any charge, unless he had some damned good reason for *wanting* to be in jail. That's the angle I can't figure out, but I know there's an angle.

Maybe the story will come out somehow, or maybe we'll never know. Ray Fleck can't tell us his end of it. Nor the psychopath his end.

For that reason only, I'm sorry I killed him. That is, I guess I am. I might have been able to subdue him without killing him, but it would have taken time. And besides there was the risk of my losing the fight. What if he'd been able to get in a lucky punch and knock me out? He'd have strangled me while I was unconscious—and then he'd have gone back to Ruth. Neither of us would have been alive right now. No, I couldn't have taken that chance.

Ruth was still unconscious when we got her to the hospital, and they gave her a sedative so she'd stay that way a while, or rather so the unconsciousness would blend into normal sleep.

So I haven't talked to her yet. They told me she should have at least a few hours of normal sleep, and kicked me out. I can go back at five A.M.

So I have a couple of hours to kill and that's what I'm doing now, writing this.

Perry, how'd you like to be my best man? Maybe I'm overconfident, but I don't think so. I'm almost certain that Ruth will marry me, now that she's free. I don't know how soon; there'll have to be what people call a decent interval. And it'll be up to Ruth how long that is. As far as I'm concerned, I'd marry her tomorrow and start out our honeymoon by attending Ray Fleck's funeral. She'd hardly go along with that, but she didn't really love him any more and

I'm hoping she'll think that not over a few months will be long enough.

And I'm serious about the best man business. And if Ruth will accept my plans, you wouldn't even have to come here to do the job. I've been thinking for a long time of taking a vacation and a trip to Europe; I'd probably have done it before now if I hadn't fallen in love with Ruth and wanted to stick around for that reason. And combining a European tour with a honeymoon would be combining pleasure with pleasure. We could be married in New York en route, so you could stand up for us there, stay a week for a look at New York if Ruth wants to (and I imagine she will; she's never been there) and then hop off for Europe.

I feel as though I'm dreaming, and I suppose I am—but it's a dream that wilt come true, I know it will.

Your old friend,

G M

George Mikos

NO ORCHIDS FOR MISS BLANDISH

JAMES HADLEY CHASE

FLESH
OF THE
ORCHID

crazy \'kra ze\ adj,

JAMES
HADLEY
CHASE

A raucous thrill ride of a novel and sequel to the classic crime novel, *NO ORCHIDS FOR MISS BLANDISH*. The story bristles with crazy plot twists, edge-of-the-seat suspense and a cast of intriguing low-life's who mix it up for an immensely enjoyable read.

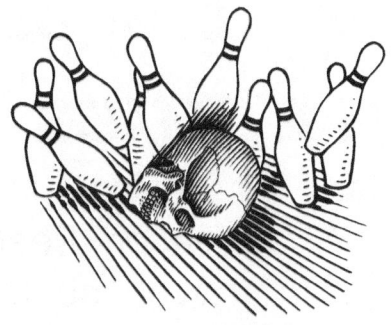

**Coming soon from
Bruin Crimeworks:**

…two thrilling novels by the
by one of the top crime writers of
any generation— *David Dodge*

DEATH & TAXES

Noir-town San Francisco is the
backdrop for this fast-paced, fresh and
flat-out enjoyable novel about tax
evasion, shattered loyalties and, of
course, murder. Whit Whitney is one
the most endearing characters to
appear in American crime fiction.

To Catch a Thief

Immortalized on film by Alfred
Hitchcock, *TO CATCH A THIEF* is a
classic romantic crime caper. This
timeless story of love and honor
unfolds amidst a high stakes game of
cat-and-mouse. Out of print and scarce
for many years, Bruin Crimeworks is
proud to make it available again.